The Parker Twins

2

Jungle Hideout

2

THE PARKER TWINS
SERIES

Jungle Hideout

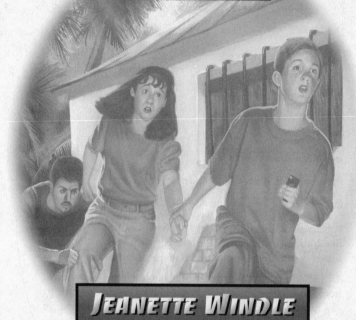

JEANETTE WINDLE

kregel
PUBLICATIONS

Grand Rapids, MI 49501

Jungle Hideout

Previously published as *Adventures in South America.*

© 1994, 1999, 2001 by Jeanette Windle

Published by Kregel Publications, a division of Kregel, Inc., P.O. Box 2607, Grand Rapids, MI 49501. For more information about Kregel Publications, visit our Web site: www.kregel.com.

ISBN 0-8254-4146-3

Printed in the United States of America

1 2 3 4 5 / 05 04 03 02 01

The Parker Twins

SERIES

2

Jungle Hideout

DANGER EVERYWHERE

ITS OUTSTRETCHED wings riding a rising current of air, the vulture watched hopefully. Its keen gaze narrowed as the tropical sun burned away the last wisp of cloud hiding the small running figure far below.

Without slowing his headlong speed, Justin brushed the sweat from his eyes with a sunburned arm that was scratched and sore from the sharp edges of man-high grasses. A long cut, ripped across one cheek by a poorly dodged bramble, stung from the salt of both sweat and tears. Wincing as a ragged tear in his jeans rubbed against a grazed knee, Justin paused to yank his T-shirt free from the stubborn grasp of a thorn bush.

His tongue was dry and swollen, and a growing pain in his side made him drag his steps, but he did his best to ignore these minor discomforts. The urgency of his errand pushed him on toward the safety of the encampment whose metal roofs floated above the brush far to his right. He wondered briefly what might be happening to Jenny right now.

Justin broke from the cover of the brush into a once-cleared field of knee-high grasses. Like a grazing herd of prehistoric beasts, oil pumps of black-painted metal dotted the landscape. Too late, he dove for cover at the sight of a tall figure who scanned the horizon only thirty feet away. Justin groaned inwardly as the other's searching eyes widened in triumph.

Justin lurched to his feet and raced away, dodging between the oil derricks. He ran more easily, now that his precious package no longer tugged at his waist. The dangerous shelter of the jungle loomed just a few yards ahead. It was his one chance of escape—if he could only outdistance the powerful runner behind him.

A shout rang out from the edge of the jungle far to his left, and Justin felt a surge of hope as he saw the hazy outline of a man motioning in his direction. But an answering shout came from behind him, and hope turned to horror as Justin recognized the man who sprinted along the jungle edge to cut him off.

With a last, desperate burst of speed, Justin crashed into the dense cover of the jungle only yards ahead of his two pursuers. Instantly he froze, forgetting the danger behind him. Like a single frame from an old silent movie, every detail of the scene before him impressed itself upon his memory.

Unfamiliar trees formed a canopy here that shut out the relentless glare of the tropical sun. Vines as big around as Justin's arm roped the trees together in an almost impenetrable tangle. Countless varieties of orchids dripped from branches and spilled down tree trunks to splash drops of color across the watery-green gloom.

A gigantic downed tree of some exotic redwood lay across his path, the charred trunk giving evidence of the lightning storm that had caused its fall. A shaft of sunshine explored the opening the tree had left in the dense canopy, and danced across the tiny clearing. At the center of the setting was the great animal, crouched unmoving on padded feet. The light that glinted across its back was no brighter than the dappled pelt.

In the background, an orchestra of jungle sounds played an accompaniment to the dreamlike scene. A guacamaya, the great rainbow-colored parrot of the tropics, called loudly overhead to its mate. A troop of chattering brown monkeys gossiped among the branches. A bright green tree frog, its touch carrying a deadly poison, whistled through the air to land with a splat on a tree trunk above Justin's head. And underlying the jungle music was the rhythmic, almost purring rumble of the great beast—which now eyed the motionless boy with growing interest.

The loud snap of a branch broke the spell of the frozen moment. The low purr rose to an angry roar. A short tail lashed the ground in fury as powerful muscles bunched under the sleek skin. Justin's hands felt the sticky sap of the tree trunk at his back. Breathing deeply to control his fear, he glanced around, but he saw no hope of escape. Whispering a desperate prayer, he shut his eyes, just as the great gold-and-black animal launched itself into the air.

Chapter One

AN UNUSUAL BUS RIDE

JUSTIN PARKER scowled down at the half-closed suitcase on the bedroom floor. Tucking in the escaping sleeve of a blue shirt, he forced the stuffed case together. Gripping the bulging sides between his legs, the tall, husky thirteen-year-old snapped the clasps shut before the contents could escape again.

Running his fingers through red-gold hair that would have curled if he hadn't kept it so short, he glanced around at the one empty suitcase and the chaos that still covered the floor.

"Where did all this junk come from, anyway?" he demanded. "I know it all fit in here before!"

Pushing dark curls back from a flushed face, Justin's twin sister, Jenny, shoved a heap of winter clothing into a duffel bag before answering, "Who was it that insisted on buying all those souvenirs this morning? That llama-skin rug took up half the suitcase!"

Justin's blue-green eyes twinkled as he protested, "*You* were the one who had to buy alpaca sweaters for everyone and his dog!"

Golden eyes flashing fire, Jenny jumped to her feet. Hands

on hips, she exploded, "Uncle Pete said we could get some presents for Mom and Dad and the rest of the family! Besides, he gave me a duffel bag so I wouldn't take up any extra room in the suitcase. . . ."

Seeing the wide grin on her brother's freckled face, she realized she was being teased. With an exasperated frown, she grabbed a pillow and threw it at him.

Justin and Jenny Parker were as different in character as they were in appearance. Though Justin was usually calm and even-tempered, friends soon recognized a certain stubborn set of his jaw. Hazel eyes took in everything around him, and a scientific aptitude led him to investigate anything unusual.

Jenny was as outgoing and talkative as her brother was steady, but a strong streak of common sense balanced her excitable temperament. In spite of their differences, they were the best of friends—most of the time.

"Hey! Careful with the camera!" Kicking the pillow aside, Justin picked their small camera up off the floor. Slinging the camera strap around his neck, Justin leaned down to pick up a large, colored envelope that had been lying underneath.

"What's that?" Jenny reached for the envelope. Justin batted her hand away and slowly studied the writing on the front. Turning the envelope over and over, he carefully examined every inch until Jenny nearly danced with impatience.

"Don't be mean, Justin!" she pleaded. "Open it!"

With a teasing grin, Justin relented, slit the top of the envelope with his penknife, and pulled out a stack of photos.

"Our pictures!" Jenny squealed. Looking over his shoulder, she exclaimed, "Look, there's Lake Titicaca and the balsa boats.

And there's Tiawanaku . . . and the Gate to the Sun with Pedro and me standing in front. And . . . and there's the cave!"

She shuddered at a picture of what looked like a high, manmade mound. A dark opening in the hillside promised entrance, but a closer look revealed that the opening had been bricked shut.

Justin and Jenny Parker had arrived in La Paz, the capital city of Bolivia, less than a week before. Their uncle—whose job required that he fly all over the world troubleshooting for Triton Oil, an international oil company—had invited the twins to spend their summer vacation with him. He planned to combine some business with holiday sightseeing.

During their few days in La Paz, the two children had stumbled onto a gang of criminals who smuggled ancient Inca artifacts out of the country. Taken captive by the smugglers, Justin and Jenny had escaped among the ruins. Only the power of God had rescued them from the cave and brought about the capture of the smugglers.

Justin quickly stuffed the pictures back into their envelope as the door swung open. A tall man obviously related to Justin walked in. A red-headed Santa Claus, Pete Parker liked to blame his size on the hospitality he couldn't refuse in the countries he visited all over the world. Now he raised reddish-brown eyebrows at the mess on the floor.

"Aren't you two done packing? We leave for the airport in just two hours. Mrs. Evans has lunch waiting downstairs." The Evanses were the young missionary couple who had made the three Parkers welcome during their stay in La Paz.

"We're almost ready, Uncle Pete," the twins said together,

hurriedly shoving the rest of their belongings into the remaining suitcase.

"Did you remember to keep your summer clothes separate? It may be winter up here in the mountains, but it's always hot in the Beni." Since Bolivia was south of the equator, seasons were reversed. The Parker twins had left behind summer in their home city of Seattle to find themselves in the middle of the cold season here. Now finished with his business in La Paz, Uncle Pete had been asked to check out a shutdown in an oil camp in the Beni, Bolivia's tropical jungle area.

Several hours later, in the spacious airport lobby of the Bolivian lowland city of Santa Cruz, Jenny plopped down on top of her suitcase. "Can you believe it was winter just an hour ago?" she panted, pulling off her jacket.

Justin wiped his face with an already damp handkerchief and tugged unhappily at the high-necked sweater he'd put on that morning. "Uncle Pete says it's even hotter in the Beni!"

Jenny groaned. Just then Uncle Pete, a frown knitting his eyebrows, hurried over from the information desk. "Sorry, kids! It looks like our flight to the Beni got bumped. It'll be three days before the next flight. I guess we'd better find a hotel."

This time it was Justin who groaned. "Oh, Uncle Pete! Isn't there some other way we could go?"

Uncle Pete looked doubtful. "Well, there is the bus. But it's an eighteen-hour trip."

"I like bus *travel!*" Justin declared cheerfully. "Let's go for it!"

"Yeah, we took the bus to California last summer," Jenny agreed. "It was fun!"

"If you think you can handle it, that'll suit me fine! I'll telegraph the oil camp of our change of plans." His blue-green eyes crinkled in fun as Uncle Pete added, "But I'm warning you, this won't be like any bus ride you've ever had!"

The sun was setting by the time a battered taxi let them off at the bus terminal on the far side of Santa Cruz. "This doesn't look so bad." Justin declared as they watched their suitcases disappear under the heaped-up luggage on top of a bus much like a city bus back home. "Of course there isn't a bathroom, but I think it'll be lots of fun!"

Justin wondered about Uncle Pete's quick chuckle. Glancing up, he caught a look of mischief he'd seen before—when his dad had smuggled salt into Mom's sugar bowl last April Fool's Day.

"What does he know that we don't?" Justin whispered to Jenny as they threaded their way to seats in the back. Uncle Pete squeezed in beside a farmer several rows ahead of them. By the time they had settled in, the rest of the seats were filled up, but passengers continued to crowd onto the bus.

"Where do they think they're going to sit?" Jenny asked curiously.

She soon found out as a heavy woman dropped a large bundle into the narrow aisle beside the twins. Collapsing on top of the bundle, she pulled her thin cotton dress down over fat knees. Her plump, sweaty arm pressed against Justin as she tried to make herself comfortable in the too-narrow space.

As Justin edged away, a squawk startled both children. Peering over the high back of their seat, they saw several chickens, their feet tied together, resting on a teenage girl's lap.

The sun had now disappeared behind the city, and Justin reached up to flick on the overhead light. It didn't work. Standing up, he looked along the length of the bus. Every square inch of the aisle was now packed with standing or sitting passengers. Small children crowded in with those passengers fortunate enough to find seats.

A loud snuffle at Justin's feet whirled him around. Jenny hurriedly lifted her feet up as she exclaimed, "Hey, it's a baby pig!"

"*Disculpa*," a timid voice said, interrupting their amazed stare. A small, dark-haired boy dragged the piglet out from under the seat. With an apologetic smile, he disappeared down the aisle.

"It's going to be a long night at this rate!" Justin growled as the last of the light disappeared. "I guess we might as well get some sleep."

He soon discovered that this wasn't going to be easy. As they left behind the paved streets of the city, ear-deafening rock music blasted from two ancient speakers at the front of the bus. The twins clung to their seats as the road became a pair of bone-rattling ruts.

Justin tried the recliner button on the armrest, but that didn't work either. Finally, the twins wadded up their jackets as pillows and leaned against each other to rest as best they could.

Justin was in an uneasy sleep when a sudden jolt threw him to the floor. Picking himself up, he realized that the bus had stopped and was tilting dangerously. A glance at his luminous watch face told him it was two A.M.

Jenny rubbed her eyes sleepily. "What's wrong?" she asked anxiously.

Justin peered out the window. An earlier rain had churned a low spot in the dirt road into a sloppy mud hole. By the rising moon, he could see that the bus tires were buried to the hubcaps in mud.

"I think we're stuck!" he answered. "Come on!"

By now the bus was in an uproar as passengers grabbed their belongings and pushed their way toward the door. Justin and Jenny carefully picked their way down the now sharply slanting aisle to the open door, and jumped across to a grassy area. The tires on this side rested on the solid road edge, causing the bus to list heavily to one side.

Men were already lifting down the heavy luggage from the top of the bus, while others tried to dig out the embedded tires. The bus driver called out orders over the crying of young children. Uncle Pete rolled up his pant legs and took a turn with a shovel, while the twins joined the women and older children in searching for stones and heavy pieces of wood to shove under the bus tires.

An hour later, the bus finally lumbered free of the clinging mud. Dirty and exhausted, the twins made their way back to their seats, only to find the heavy woman replaced by the small boy and his pig. The piglet's squeals ended their attempts to sleep.

Noon was long gone when the bus finally jolted into Trinidad, capital of the Beni, and pulled up in front of a small, redbrick terminal. Uncle Pete caught Jenny as she stumbled stiffly off the bus. Rubbing his hunched back, Justin hobbled down the steps. "Boy, what a night!"

A grin split the red beard. "Didn't you say it would be fun?"

"Well, it wasn't exactly *fun*," Justin answered, as he loosened dried mud from his pant legs. Remembering one of his dad's favorite expressions, he added, "But it certainly was an educational experience!"

Jenny dropped her backpack and fanned her face with a magazine. "You were right about one thing, Uncle Pete. This *is* even hotter than Santa Cruz!"

Porters were already lifting luggage down from the top of the bus, and a crowd of welcoming relatives and candy vendors pressed around the passengers. Uncle Pete looked around. "I don't see any Americans. Someone from the oil camp should be here to pick us up."

Justin had lifted the last of their suitcases from the pile of luggage when he noticed a slim, very blond young man half-running across the terminal. Pleasant sunburned features looked accustomed to smiling, but at the moment the man looked worried. His frown went away when he caught sight of the Parkers, and he waved over the crowd of dark heads.

The young man looked flustered as he squeezed his way through to the Parkers. Pushing his hair back from his eyes, he apologized, "Sorry I'm late. We haven't made a mail run for over a week, and I just picked up your telegram, as well as the telegram from headquarters. I was afraid I'd missed you. Just as well, I guess—the bus was late, as usual."

Still breathless, he thrust out a hand. "I forgot to introduce myself. Alan Green at your service. I oversee the Triton Oil camp here. You must be Pete Parker."

"Yes. Thanks for picking us up." Shaking the young man's

hand, Uncle Pete introduced the twins, then added, "I'm sorry you had such short notice. I imagine the telegram from headquarters mentioned their concern about the shutdown of oil production at the camp."

Under his sunburn, Mr. Green flushed with sudden annoyance. "Yes, of course. We sent in a full report about the *temporary* shutdown," he emphasized. "But we sure didn't expect an on-site investigation. As our report stated, we have things well under control."

"That may be," Uncle Pete answered pleasantly, "but as I was already in the country, the head office asked me to check out the problem personally. I hope our unexpected arrival is no inconvenience."

"Well, actually things are a bit difficult. . . ." Mr. Green looked even more flustered than before. "I mean, we weren't expecting visitors. . . . Things are very . . ."

As he trailed off, Jenny whispered loudly to Justin, "He acts just like you do when Mom pulls a surprise room check!"

Justin grinned but stepped on her foot warningly as Mr. Green glanced back at the two children. Uncle Pete picked up a suitcase in each hand. "The kids and I are prepared to rough it," he said reassuringly. But his tone was firm as he added, "Why don't we continue this discussion on our way?"

Still looking unhappy, the camp administrator picked up the two remaining bags and led the way to an open, four-wheel-drive jeep. Justin noticed the insignia of Triton Oil painted on both doors. Once the luggage was settled in the back of the jeep, Mr. Green turned to Uncle Pete. "I'll be making a brief stop in town. It's a two-hour drive out to camp. I need to pick up some supplies, and you'll probably want a bite to eat before we head out."

As they left the terminal, they turned onto a wide, cobblestone street bordered by one-story houses of adobe brick. Fresh coats of whitewash shimmered in the sun. There was little traffic in the streets. Both pedestrians and cattle ambled down the center of the road, seemingly unaware as cars whizzed by.

"Is this really the capital city, Mr. Green?" Jenny asked doubtfully, as they dodged a small cart pulled by two sturdy oxen. "It seems so small!"

The camp administrator's expression brightened as he glanced back at Jenny's eager face. He pulled up beside a small central plaza before answering. "Yes, Trinidad is the capital of the Beni. It isn't very big, but then the Beni doesn't have a large population. It's a lot like the old American West. You'll find a lot more cattle, snakes, and monkeys around here than you will people . . . not to mention every kind of bug you can imagine."

Justin's freckled face lit up. "Wow! It sounds like my kind of country, Mr. Green."

The young man smiled slightly. "I like it too. And you can call me Alan, okay?"

He opened the driver's door of the jeep and stepped out. "This is where we get out. The open-air market is a block down that way." He gestured down a narrow side street.

"You have about an hour for sightseeing—unless you'd rather come with me to the market."

Jenny was already at his side. "I'll go with you. I've never seen a real open-air market."

"Yeah, I'm coming too!" Justin agreed.

The three Parkers followed Alan down the dusty alley. Overhanging balconies blocked much of the light. The twins blinked as the gloom opened into a blaze of color. Plastic awnings of red, green, and blue provided shade for piles of every kind of goods. Black-haired women in bright cotton dresses lazily swished insects away from their produce. A roar of buyers bargained over the price of ripe bananas or fresh corn.

On Alan's heels, the Parkers threaded through the narrow footpaths between stands. Jenny stared with fascination at the baskets of tropical fruit: green and orange papayas, bright yellow mangoes speckled with brown, pineapples, pale stalks of sugar cane peeled and ready to chew.

Uncle Pete moved away to examine a pile of supposedly genuine Swiss watches, while Alan bargained for fresh produce. Justin fingered a round, green object the size of a cantaloupe piled among other exotic fruits. "What's this called?"

Alan shrugged. "That's just an avocado."

Justin looked closely. "Boy, you sure don't see them this big back home!"

"Hey, take a look at these!" Jenny called.

At the next stand a young Indian woman nursed a toddler while she fanned small hills of every imaginable spice: black and red pepper, cumin, bay leaves, oregano, garlic, paprika, turmeric. A basket piled high with diamond-shaped green leaves caught Justin's attention. They didn't look like any herb he had ever seen. He raised his camera to snap a picture of the strange leaf when a tap on his shoulder whirled him around.

In front of him stood an old man. Deep wrinkles crisscrossed his gaunt face, but the oily strands that hung below a threadbare hat were still black. One cheek bulged. Wiping a claw-like hand across his mouth, he spat sideways, spraying Justin's Nikes with a stream of green.

With a frown, Justin stepped back, wiping his shoes against a patch of grass. Hitching up well-patched pants belted with a piece of rope, the old man grabbed Justin's arm and pointed to the basket of green leaves.

"What does he want?" Justin asked, glancing frantically around for Alan.

He shrugged his shoulders helplessly as the old man continued to babble. But Alan suddenly stepped between the children and the old man, a frown on his face as he answered emphatically in Spanish. The only word Justin recognized was "No!"

"The poor old man! I think he just wants something to eat!"

At the sound of Jenny's voice, the old man held out a thin hand in her direction. He eagerly grabbed a handful of green leaves from the basket and motioned toward them. Jenny already had her coin purse open when Alan shook his head sharply.

"You don't want any of that!" he informed her curtly.

"Why not?" Justin asked curiously, "What is that stuff, anyway?"

Alan's short laugh held no humor as he gently removed the leaves from the old man's hand and replaced them with a handful of bananas. "You still don't know what this is? You really are *gringos!*"

Eyeing the bananas with scorn, the beggar shuffled away. Alan tossed the diamond-shaped leaves back into the basket. "That, kids, is coca leaf! That old man is a coca chewer."

"Oh!" Jenny said with interest. "You mean, like the coca tea they gave me in La Paz for high altitude sickness."

"That's right," Alan nodded. "One of its more legitimate uses. What that man wants it for isn't quite so healthy. More importantly, it's from these innocent-looking green leaves—including plenty from this very market—that cocaine is made. Bolivia's 'white gold'."

Chapter Two

SURPRISE AT THE OIL CAMP

"MR. GREEN—I mean, uh . . . Alan—that old man back there. Was it chewing those coca leaves that did that to him?" asked Jenny. "And if it's so bad for you, why are they selling it in the market like that? Isn't it illegal or something?"

They were bumping along a dusty track cut through thick brush. Deep ruts showed where the rains had washed out the one-lane road. Palm trees dotted unfenced grasslands where cattle grazed, and bottle trees looked like giant brown vases topped with a cluster of leafy branches, instead of flowers. Occasionally they passed a bamboo shack with a roof of palm leaves.

The young oil worker hunched over the steering wheel, his expression still tense and worried. He seemed not to have heard her question, so Jenny repeated it. Glancing up into the rearview mirror, Alan answered, "Actually, it's perfectly legal to grow and sell coca in Bolivia."

Surprised, Jenny demanded, "But—then it isn't bad for you? I mean, chewing it like that old man!"

Alan drove around a deep pothole, then said seriously, "Well, yes and no! Chewing the coca leaf keeps you from feeling hunger or cold or tiredness—that's why so many poor people chew it. But when it wears off, you're just that much more tired and hungry. If you keep feeding your body coca instead of the food and rest it really needs, eventually your body will break down like a car that doesn't get the gas and oil it needs. And after awhile it destroys your ability to think and work. If you keep it up long enough, you end up like that old man."

Justin joined in. "Why do they keep chewing it, then?"

Alan shrugged. "Why do Americans keep smoking when they know it's bad for them? It's hard to change things when these people have been growing and chewing coca for hundreds of years. Anyway, now Bolivia has a problem that's a lot bigger than coca."

He swerved suddenly to avoid a herd of long-horned steers that burst into the road. "Sorry!" Looking back, he continued, "How much do you kids know about cocaine?"

Justin hesitated a moment. "What we learn at school, I guess. They're always having special programs and police coming in to talk about drugs. Cocaine comes from South America, and drug dealers smuggle it into the U.S., right? Kids take it maybe only once, and then they get addicted so they can't *stop* taking it."

"Yeah, so if someone offers it to you, you just tell them NO!" Jenny added forcefully.

A sudden smile transformed Alan's face. "You've got *that* right! The problem is, some kids *don't* say no."

"Which I hope will never be you two!" Uncle Pete put in sternly. "You saw what coca did to that old man. Cocaine is concentrated from the coca leaves and is a thousand times more powerful. Too many kids try it just to be 'cool,' or because some so-called friend talks them into it. It gives them a good feeling for a little while, but eventually they discover they're not more popular or cool—just *addicted.* It doesn't take long before they find they can't live without cocaine."

Alan added sadly, "Addicts will do anything—steal or even kill—to get money to buy cocaine. That's why it's called 'white gold'—because it's worth as much as gold to the people who buy and sell it. I saw too many of my high school friends ruin their lives with drugs. That's why . . ."

Alan glanced at Uncle Pete. The worried look was again on his face. But Justin and Jenny had turned their attention to the scenery. They were now moving out of the grasslands.

Here the brush gave way to towering trees. Vines as thick as a man's wrist twisted around branches and hung down into the jeep.

Overhead chattered whole colonies of brightly colored birds. Justin caught sight of a red, green, and black parrot fluttering from branch to branch. He was disappointed, though, not to see any of the exotic jungle animals he had read about and seen in zoos.

He leaned forward to ask, but Jenny took the words out of his mouth. "Where are all the monkeys and tigers, and those giant snakes?" she demanded.

Alan shook his head. "Too much of this area has been cleared for cattle. If you want to see real wildlife, you'll have to get your uncle to take you into the uncleared jungle."

Jenny leaned over the seat and hugged Uncle Pete around the neck. "Oh, Uncle Pete, would you?"

"Hey, this is a work trip, remember?" His eyes twinkled at the sight of their crestfallen faces. "But we'll try to get in one trip to the jungle."

Just then Alan slammed on the brakes as a strange animal burst into the road. The size of a pig, its long body was covered with short brown hair. Its red eyes glared down a pointed snout as it crashed into the brush and disappeared.

"Wow!" Justin exclaimed. "What was that?"

"That," Alan said as he shifted back into gear, "was a *jochi,* a kind of wild boar. It's actually of the rodent family."

Jenny gave a horrified gasp. "Rodent! You mean it's a giant rat?"

Alan chuckled. "That's right! But it makes good eating just like homegrown pork."

Jenny shuddered, but Justin sat back with a grin of pleasure. He had finally left civilization behind.

An hour later, the trees opened up into a thick brush land. A barbwire fence ran alongside the road, broken by a padlocked gate. On the other side of the gate, several acres of brush had been cleared.

"The oil camp," Alan announced as he unlocked the gate and drove the jeep through.

The twins looked around curiously. Several small bungalows with red-tile roofs lined one side of the driveway, each with an identical veranda running around it. On the other side, two larger, whitewashed buildings appeared to be offices of some sort. Beyond the buildings, they glimpsed several oil pumps, their black heads rising above the uncut brush.

As Justin jumped out of the jeep, the loud whine of an

approaching aircraft caught his attention. Shielding his eyes with one hand, he stared up as a small helicopter dropped over their heads and disappeared into the uncut brush behind the buildings.

"So Dr. Latour and Rodrigo are finally back," Alan commented. He turned to Uncle Pete.

"Dr. Latour is our chief geologist and the only other American in the camp at the moment. His assistant, Rodrigo, is the camp chemist. They've both been out all week on an oil exploration survey."

He gestured toward the unmoving oil pumps the twins had noticed and added gloomily, "In fact, except for the camp cook, they're the only others here at all, now that the oil pumps have been shut down."

He looked at Uncle Pete anxiously. "You said you knew about that."

"That's why I'm here," Uncle Pete answered pleasantly. "As I mentioned, my orders are to investigate the shutdown of production and make a recommendation as to the future of this camp. But we'll discuss that later."

Lifting out their luggage, the three Parkers followed Alan toward the nearest bungalow. Stepping onto the veranda, Alan threw open a screened door.

"These are our sleeping quarters," he told them. "This one will be yours during your stay."

He motioned to an open door in one wall that revealed another small room. "Jenny can use that for her bedroom."

Justin set down the duffel bag he carried and looked around the simple building. The floor was of rough cement, and camp beds lined the far wall. A simple closet had been made out of packing crates with a curtain over the front. What interested Justin most were the muslin nets that hung from the ceiling, making of each bed a private tent.

"Those are mosquito nets," Alan said, answering Justin's unspoken question. "Be sure to tuck them in around your bed at night. The mosquitoes around here carry malaria."

From the wide, screened window on the back wall, he pointed out a tiny wood structure about a hundred yards beyond the bungalow. "We don't have indoor plumbing, but we keep the outhouse clean. Just make sure you take your flashlight along at night, and keep the door shut against bugs and snakes."

He headed for the door, then paused. "Oh, and don't forget to shake out your shoes and clothes when you get dressed in the morning. They're favorite hiding places for scorpions."

Jenny edged closer to Justin and whispered. "I'm not so sure I'm going to like this place."

Alan was already on the veranda. "Now if you'll follow me, I'll give you a tour of camp."

As they walked leisurely around the oil camp, Alan showed the Parkers his own quarters—larger than their own, and with a kitchen added on to one side. The camp cook, wrapped in a large white apron, came to the kitchen door and greeted them in smiling Spanish.

"Our dining room," Alan commented, motioning toward several tables scattered around the veranda.

The administration office, one of the two bigger buildings on the other side of the gravel road, was one big room—cement floors and whitewashed walls like the sleeping quarters, but otherwise like any office the world over. There were files and desks and a computer, and on a table against the back wall the square black box of a two-way radio.

"A UHF radio," Alan explained. "We use it to keep in touch with exploration teams and outlying oil sites. We're out of range of telephone or even cell-phone service out here, so the UHF radio is the DEA agent communications network in the jungle. But we're not totally out of touch with modern technology."

He nodded toward the computer, which was at the moment covered with a clear plastic tarp to protect it against the dust that was thick everywhere in the room. "We have a generator that supplies electricity for the computer and other equipment as well as lights for the sleeping quarters at night. We even have Internet and e-mail, thanks to a satellite dish on the roof that allows us to uplink by cell-phone into the regular phone service in Trinidad or Santa Cruz."

As they left the office, Alan pointed out the satellite dish up on the red tile roof. It looked just like the one Justin and Jenny's dad had installed on their own roof for satellite TV. Beyond the office was another long, low building that was protected by metal bars over the windows. Its heavy wooden shutters and metal door were shut tight.

"What's in there?" Jenny asked with her usual curiosity.

"That's the lab," Alan explained. "It's where we process soil samples, among other things."

Justin was always interested in anything scientific. He asked eagerly, "Do you mind if I look around?"

At Alan's nod, Justin hurried across the gravel driveway and up the cement steps. But as he reached for the metal latch, an angry voice shouted, "Get away from there, kid!"

Stumbling backward in surprise, Justin stared up at the man who had appeared around the side of the cinder-block building. Tall and broad, with silvering dark hair, he could pass for Spanish descent. But the man's speech was pure American. His good-looking features were flushed with anger, until he noticed the two adults who stepped up behind Justin.

"What's the problem, Gerard?" Alan asked quietly.

Changing expression, the strange man answered, "I beg your pardon. I thought someone was breaking into the lab, that's all. There's a lot of dangerous chemicals lying around in there."

He looked at the Parkers. "Who are your visitors, Green?"

"This is Pete Parker and his nephew and niece, Justin and Jenny," Alan introduced. He added, "Mr. Parker is here from the head office . . . to investigate the camp."

A glint of anger showed in the cool, gray eyes. "So they think we need investigating, do they? Why wasn't I told about this visit?"

"I didn't know myself until this morning," Alan answered. "In fact, I almost missed picking them up."

Alan smiled down at Justin and Jenny. "These two would like to see the lab. You don't mind, do you?"

Dr. Latour hesitated noticeably, then swung open the heavy metal door. "Of course not. Let me show you around."

Tiled counters, littered with the usual beakers, microscopes, bottles, and other apparatus of a science lab, ran around three walls of the long room. A short, slim man stood at one counter, long black hair flopping into his eyes as he scribbled in a small ledger. At the sound of footsteps, he shoved the ledger into a drawer.

Dr. Latour waved toward the other man. "Rodrigo Ventiades."

Turning around, the Bolivian chemist took in the group of visitors. His dark face beaming pleasure, he threw his hands into the air. "But how good it is to have guests. And a lady, too!"

"Rodrigo, the Parkers are staying a few days. They'd like a *brief* look at the lab," he stressed, "before they tour the rest of the camp."

Looking around, Justin noticed a large open briefcase sitting on the nearest counter, with what looked like a combination of a touch phone and computer keyboard inside.

Alan noticed it too. "A sat-phone, Gerard? When did you get that? What's wrong with the set-up we've got in the office?"

Justin studied the complex equipment inside the briefcase admiringly. "Wow, you mean, that's one of those satellite phones you read about that can reach anywhere in the world from the middle of the desert or jungle or whatever?"

Looking displeased, Dr. Latour answered Alan. "There's nothing wrong with your set-up, if you want to carry those UHF radios every time you step off base. Besides, like the kid says, with this I don't have to wait to get back in range of that satellite dish of yours to make a phone call. You might think of ditching those old radios for a couple of these yourself."

"Sure, if we had a few thousand extra dollars! You know the budget doesn't allow for that, especially now! Still, if you want to spend your own money, it's your wallet, not mine."

His angry face growing darker, Dr. Latour swung around sharply on the camp administrator, but before he could retort, Rodrigo hurriedly stepped forward. Taking Jenny's hand, he bowed and said, "You are very welcome here. I only regret that

I cannot accompany you on your tour of this site. We have just returned from a long trip, and there is much to do."

"Then get back to work!" the geologist ordered curtly as Jenny giggled. Turning to the others, he added abruptly, "We have this week's surveys to process, so if you'll please excuse us. . . ."

Alan led the Parkers away from the lab. "Sorry about that! Gerard isn't the friendliest man."

"I'll say he isn't!" Justin muttered to Jenny.

Alan continued, "He's a brilliant geologist, though. We're fortunate to have him here. They say he can actually smell out oil."

"Did he discover *this* field?" Uncle Pete asked.

"No, this site was discovered by an earlier team. After the camp was set up, Dr. Latour came in to take charge of exploration and development. He's only been with Triton a few months, but he's lived in Bolivia for years. He has a lot of friends in high places here. He even won a medal from the Bolivian government—the 'Condor of the Andes,' their highest honor—for his work in uncovering new oil fields. Not that he's had much luck here!" he added gloomily.

"What about Rodrigo?" Jenny asked curiously. "He sure speaks good English."

"Dr. Latour brought him along when he came. He lived in Miami for a few years. They take care of the scientific side of things. I just keep camp life running smoothly."

He grinned down at the two children. "Not very exciting, huh?"

But he had just lost the attention of his audience. "What in the world is that?" the twins exclaimed together.

Rounding the corner of the lab, they had come out on the edge of the uncut brush that bordered the camp. The twins stared in astonishment at what looked like a full-scale military encampment dropped into the brush. Though several hundred yards away, it was still inside the barbwire fence that bordered Triton property.

Army tents sat beside a prefabricated, dome-shaped aluminum hut. The grass had been clipped short around the hut, and two men in khaki uniforms stood at attention on either side of the entrance. A half-dozen American army jeeps and one large transport truck lined one side of the encampment.

Justin's eyes opened wider as he noticed a real combat helicopter resting in a clearing beside the large hut. The long rotor blades glinted in the setting sun.

"What, exactly, is going on here, Alan?" Uncle Pete asked sternly. "I wasn't told about any military operation on Triton property. I doubt if headquarters knows either or they would have informed me."

"I . . . I know, sir! I was going to let them know." Alan looked very unhappy. "It's just a DEA camp."

"A DEA camp? You mean the Drug Enforcement Agency?" Uncle Pete raised his eyebrows in amazement. "What is it doing here?"

"It . . . it's like this," Alan explained hastily. "I usually go up to Santa Cruz when I have time off. You kind of get to know the other Americans . . . you know, at embassy parties and all. That's how I met Special Agent Turner. He's with the DEA—their Resident-Agent-in-Charge, as they call their head of operations, of the Santa Cruz field office. I got to know him pretty well—stayed with him a couple of times—and I . . . I told him he was welcome to stay here if he ever came to the Beni.

"I meant on his time off, but last week he called me up on the radio and told me the Bolivian government had finally given him permission to run an operation down here. He asked if my offer was still open. . . ."

Alan flushed red to the roots of his ash-blond hair. "There wasn't time to go through the red tape at headquarters, and I didn't think anyone would mind. . . . I mean, everything was shut up here anyway . . . so I said fine!"

He waved toward the encampment. "They came down two days ago. I didn't know there'd be so many of them. Then I found out you were coming. . . ."

Looking as unhappy as when he had met them at the bus station, he added gloomily, "Doug—uh, Special Agent Turner isn't going to be very happy about this. I told him he wouldn't have to worry about visitors. I guess I'm in trouble all the way around!"

The twins waited anxiously as Uncle Pete studied the encampment. They already liked the young camp administrator. After a long moment, Uncle Pete said thoughtfully, "I don't see any problem with them using the property. You did exceed your authority, and you'd better ask first next time, but I'll let the head office know I okayed it."

As Alan broke into a relieved smile, Justin asked, "Could we go see the helicopter?"

Alan nodded. "I guess I'd better let Doug know you're here. Come on."

The party of four threaded their way single-file along a narrow path trampled through the brush. When they reached the edge of the other camp, they found themselves surrounded by armed men in the uniform of the Bolivian army.

"*Son amigos*," a voice called from the hut. The soldiers relaxed their weapons as a short, stocky man in civilian clothing stepped outside. A gray crewcut set off his tan.

"That's Special Agent Turner," Alan explained quickly as the DEA agent walked over.

The American law officer looked at Alan sharply. "I understood there'd be no visitors."

He listened with a frown as Alan tried to explain.

"Well, it can't be helped now!" Special Agent Turner interrupted, cutting off Alan's apologies. Keen gray eyes studied the group for a long moment, then he held out a hand to Uncle Pete.

"Special Agent Doug Turner at your service. Please forgive me for the short welcome. We're trying to keep casual visitors out of the area, but I don't think you'll create a problem as long as you let us know when you leave. I trust you won't mind if we check out your credentials." At Uncle Pete's nod of agreement, he waved the group toward the hut.

High screens divided the interior of the aluminum building into several work areas. The central section was jammed with office equipment, computer stations, and other instruments the children couldn't identify. A tall young man barely out of his teens bent over what Justin guessed to be a radar screen, a headset topping his close-cropped, dark curls.

Special Agent Turner pulled out some folding chairs and bellowed, "Mike, we've got company! Turn around and be sociable."

The young man turned in his office chair. Black eyes widened as he saw the visitors, and he yanked off the earphones. Long, dark fingers flew over a keyboard, and the screen before him blinked off.

"Sit down! Sit down!" The DEA agent still wasn't smiling, but he seemed a little more friendly. "Mike, why don't you bring some coffee."

As the younger man disappeared behind a screen, he added, "Mike Winters is one of my agents and the best pilot in the whole narcotics—illegal drugs—division. Now, what were your names again?"

As Uncle Pete introduced the group, Justin looked around at the fascinating equipment that filled the hut. The young pilot, Mike, brought coffee, then sat again in front of the radar screen. Justin wished he'd turn it back on, but the pilot just sat staring ahead—his broad, dark features unhappy—as Doug Turner and Uncle Pete talked. Justin eyed him curiously, then turned his attention back to the conversation.

"What exactly is your mission here?" Uncle Pete asked. "Or are you allowed to say?"

"Oh, it's no secret—not after it's been splashed across every newspaper in the country. The DEA is here on the invitation of the Bolivian government to work with their antinarcotics corps, UMOPAR."

Glancing down at the listening children, he added, "That's the Bolivian police department that deals with drugs-related crimes. The U.S. government provides the equipment, and the UMOPAR supplies the men."

The DEA agent leaned back in his chair. "We're actually down here now to teach the UMOPAR men our methods in fighting the drug trade. But if we can actually catch some drug traffickers, all the better. The Beni is a main source of cocaine shipments—billions of dollars worth.

"We were informed that there's a major cocaine smuggling ring in this area, but we haven't found any signs of it. The problem is that there are a thousand hiding places out there in the jungle. We aren't giving up, though!"

Justin noticed Mike shifting in his chair, tossing a pen from hand to hand. Suddenly he stood up. "If you'll excuse me, sir," he said in a soft drawl. "I'd like to look over tomorrow's surveillance charts."

Mike left the room abruptly as Special Agent Turner nodded agreement. The DEA agent sighed. "That boy never slows down." He, too, stood up. "He keeps us all hopping!"

As his visitors followed his lead, Special Agent Turner walked the group to the edge of camp. "I'll be having the DEA office in Santa Cruz check you out in the morning," he said as he shook Uncle Pete's hand. "Please understand this is a routine procedure." He nodded farewell and strode back toward the base.

Light clouds skittered across the face of the rising moon as they followed the path single-file back to the oil camp. At the edge of the uncut field, Justin noticed a tall, motionless figure outlined in the light of an unshuttered lab window. Dr. Latour was staring in disbelief at the DEA encampment.

As Alan stepped onto the cut grass, the geologist demanded with cold anger, "I demand to know the meaning of this, Green!"

He checked himself as Uncle Pete followed Alan into the rectangle of light, then added more calmly, "What is the Bolivian army doing squatting on our land?"

"It's a DEA camp," Alan explained again.

"A what?" Dr. Latour shouted.

"You know, the DEA people I met in Santa Cruz," Alan said patiently. "I've mentioned them before."

"What are they doing *here?*"

"Special Agent Turner asked to use our camp as base, and I gave him permission. The camp is practically empty, anyway, with the pumps shut down. They called me up while you were gone this last week and set up the day before yesterday."

"You had no right to invite them here!" Justin was surprised at the fury in the geologist's voice. "Why wasn't I consulted about this?"

Alan's pleasant tones turned cool as he answered, "Gerard, you may be in charge of exploration and development, but I'm still administrator of this camp. As for consulting you, I tried to get you on the radio. You know you're supposed to keep in contact during survey trips, but you haven't checked in once all week. Besides . . ." he glanced over at Uncle Pete, "the DEA presence here has already been approved."

Dr. Latour didn't protest further, and Alan turned away. Uncle Pete and Jenny followed, but Justin looked back to where the head geologist still stared across at the twinkling lights of the DEA encampment. At that moment, the full moon broke through its cover; Justin caught his breath sharply as its silver rays touched Dr. Latour. *What is it about the DEA base that Dr. Latour hates so much?* he wondered.

Chapter Three

AN ANGRY PILOT

Wiping the juice from his chin with a cloth napkin, Justin reached for another slice of sun-ripened pineapple. "Boy, this is the best stuff I've ever eaten!"

It was early morning, and he was enjoying the typical Beni breakfast of rolls and tropical fruit. Though it was barely past dawn, a warm, moist breeze blowing across the veranda where they ate promised another scorching day.

"Where are Dr. Latour and Rodrigo?" Jenny asked, waving a sugar bun in the direction of the lab. "Don't they eat breakfast?"

Alan poured himself a cup of steaming black coffee. "Yes, I heard them out here earlier. They like to get an early start at—"

He was interrupted as Dr. Latour strode up the veranda steps. Justin studied the tall, handsome geologist curiously. Dressed in a lightweight suit and tie, he looked businesslike and confident. Justin wondered if he could have imagined the doctor's fury the night before.

"I'm on my way out," he said abruptly. "I'll be needing the helicopter again."

Alan looked surprised. "You're leaving again already? What about Mr. Parker's investigation?"

"There are important tests I need to finish," Dr. Latour explained curtly. He nodded to Uncle Pete. "I'd have made other arrangements if I'd known you were coming, but these can't wait. We'll be back tomorrow."

"I planned to take Mr. Parker up, but I guess we can wait," Alan answered pleasantly. "Just keep in touch this time."

Dr. Latour looked annoyed. "We can handle our own affairs, Green."

"I'm sure you can, but that helicopter is Triton property and my responsibility."

Without answering, Dr. Latour turned and marched away. Alan grinned at the children. Now that he was no longer worried about his unexpected visitors, his friendly personality had returned.

"Orders are that we check in at least every six hours when we're out in the bush—in case of breakdowns or some other emergency," he explained. "However, Dr. Latour is used to working on his own."

Uncle Pete set down his empty coffee cup. "Not to change the subject, but it's time we got down to business."

He motioned toward the oil pumps in the distance, black shapes against the pink remnants of the sunrise. "I'm curious to know why you shut down production. The reports we received indicated large quantities of high-grade oil."

"Yeah, we thought we had a real find here," Alan answered gloomily. "We were getting ready to bring in a whole crew of American and Bolivian personnel when Dr. Latour's tests showed that the first wells we dug were running out. What's left is too low-grade to process."

"You realize that Triton can't maintain an unprofitable camp," Uncle Pete answered with regret. "If there's no oil, we'll have to pull out of this area."

"I don't think it will come to that," Alan responded quickly. "I told you Dr. Latour is a genius at exploration. He's been working night and day to find another site. He's brought in several promising surveys. I'm sure he'll have some good results soon."

Uncle Pete stood up. "That will be taken into account. I'd like to go over those surveys and test results myself this morning."

"Sure! They're on file in the office. Dr. Latour could explain them better, but I'll do my best."

Alan quickly swallowed the rest of his coffee and followed Uncle Pete to the edge of the veranda. He turned toward the twins. "You're welcome to look around, but stay on the camp grounds and keep your eyes open. You'll find snakes and an occasional wild animal even around here."

The children spent the morning exploring the grounds, Justin snapping pictures everywhere they went. They thoroughly inspected all the buildings except the tightly shut lab. They even poked their heads into the kitchen, but the busy cook chased them out with a raised frying pan!

For an hour they watched Alan and Uncle Pete bend over the computer and shuffle through stacks of files spread out on the old, termite-chewed desk in the camp office. They lazily searched through a pile of outdated magazines, then wandered around the room, reading the captions below dusty pictures of early oil explorers. Finally, Uncle Pete ordered the restless pair out of the office.

At lunchtime the twins found the veranda table set for only two. They were just finishing their meal when they saw the cook emerge from the office with a tray of dirty dishes.

"This is *boring!*" Jenny complained as the cook cleared the table. "I thought the jungle would be exciting."

Justin pushed back his chair. "Well, I'm not staying around here any more! Come on, let's go for a walk."

Jenny agreed, and the two children paused only to grab their hats before heading toward the overgrown field beyond the camp. Watchful for snakes, they tramped their way through to a small clearing, where one of the oil pumps sat motionless. The noonday sun blazed overhead, and they were glad to rest in the shade of the pump.

"It looks like a prehistoric grasshopper," Jenny giggled. It *did* look like some overgrown insect, the long, black body of the pump suspended by a metal frame that could be spindly legs. The insect's "head," which should have been nodding up and down to pump the oil, reared sightlessly against a deep blue sky.

Settling back against the metal frame, Justin idly watched the aluminum dome of the DEA office. The sudden roar of an engine broke the silence. Barely visible above the brush, the rotor blades of the DEA helicopter began slowly rotating.

Justin sat up suddenly. "I've got an idea! Let's go visit Mr. Turner."

Jenny shook her head doubtfully. "I thought Alan told us to stay on camp property."

"That *is* camp property," Justin insisted. He desperately wanted a closer look at that helicopter. "It's inside the fence, and that makes it Triton property."

Jenny hesitated briefly, but she was bored, too. "I guess you're right. Anyway, it's better than sitting here all day."

Uniformed guards again met them at the edge of the camp, but this time they let the twins pass by as soon as they recognized them. Now that it was daylight, Justin saw that the military helicopter was painted camouflage green. Jenny clapped her hands over her ears as the roar of the powerful engine greeted them, but Justin's eyes shone as he studied the long, gleaming lines of the body.

Only a few soldiers were in sight as Justin and Jenny walked past the temporary barracks, but as they reached the helicopter pad, Special Agent Turner climbed out of the helicopter and joined them.

"Hi, kids!" he shouted over the noise, shaking their hands. "What are you up to?"

Justin had eyes only for the long, sleek machine. "That's a Huey, isn't it?"

The DEA agent smiled at his eagerness. "That's right. A little outdated, but we get the army leftovers down here. I suppose you want to take a look."

"Could we? I've never seen one up close." In answer, the DEA agent motioned toward the open door of the helicopter, and Justin and Jenny scrambled aboard.

"Wow!" Justin exclaimed as he examined the stunning layout of instruments, careful not to touch anything. "This is great! I'd *love* to fly in one of these some day."

"Perhaps we could arrange that," Special Agent Turner,

keeping a watchful eye on their explorations from the helicopter's doorway, smiled broadly as Justin's eyes widened. "Mike! Mike, get out here!" he bellowed.

Mike emerged at a run from the aluminum office building. He was dressed in a white coverall of the type pilots wear. He slid to a halt when he saw the two children.

"What are they doing here?" he demanded roughly.

Ignoring his bad humor, Special Agent Turner clapped him on the shoulder and announced jovially, "Mike, these kids have never flown in a Huey. You wouldn't mind giving them a ride, would you?"

He explained, "Mike is doing some photographic surveillance this morning. That means he will be taking pictures of the jungle. He won't mind a couple of passengers."

The look on Mike's face showed that he *did* mind, but he obviously knew his boss too well to protest. "Okay, let's go!" he ordered crossly.

Justin hesitated in the doorway "Uh . . . sir? I think we'd better let Uncle Pete know before we go anywhere."

"No problem! I'll send one of my men over to the oil camp to explain."

Justin was too excited to say more. Mike buckled himself into the pilot's seat. He curtly ordered the two children to find a seat and fasten their seatbelts. The whole body of the helicopter vibrated as the slow turning of the rotors quickened to a blur.

The noise made speech nearly impossible, but the young pilot showed the twins how to adjust a set of earphones over their ears. A tiny microphone at mouth level allowed them to talk to each other.

"Testing, testing—one, two, three!" Jenny was trying out her microphone in the copilot's seat in front of Justin. Through a small side window, Justin watched the DEA base shrink away from the helicopter. Within minutes they were skimming over unbroken jungle, the trees so thick that the ground was invisible.

Mike frowned at his instruments as the helicopter swept back and forth across the unbroken growth. "I'm taking pictures now," he explained grudgingly.

Below, a strong breeze tossed the treetops into billowing waves across an endless green sea. Justin snapped a few pictures of his own through the thick glass of the window.

After half an hour of flying, Mike announced gruffly, "I think something's down there. Hold on! I'm going down."

The helicopter dropped so suddenly that Justin felt like his stomach would wind up in his mouth! Through the window he could see a wide clearing in the jungle. Part of it seemed to be devoted to corn and other food crops, but the biggest share of the cleared land was filled with rows of a leafy green plant.

"A coca field! I'm going in for some close-up shots." The twins were startled at the anger in Mike's voice.

Slipping sideways, the helicopter turned to make several passes across the clearing. At the end of the field was a large bamboo hut with a tin roof instead of the usual thatch. As they flew over the hut, Justin caught a glimpse of some sort of vehicle parked under the tangle of trees and vines at the edge of the clearing.

A pile of leaves as high as a man was heaped beside the hut. Justin could just barely make out the tiny figure of a man spreading the green mass with a rake. He pressed his camera against the window and shot another picture.

The sudden dive of the helicopter caught Justin unaware. He grabbed his camera just before it hit the floor. Glancing toward the copilot's seat, he saw Jenny clutching tightly to the armrests.

"What's going on?" Justin shouted over the roar that penetrated his earphones. Mike's vicious swearing was the only answer as he buzzed the bamboo hut so low that several figures scattered and ran for the protection of the jungle that surrounded the field.

"Mike, please! What's the matter?" Jenny asked in a voice that trembled as the helicopter pulled out of its dive and turned back over the jungle.

The bitter lines on the dark young face deepened as Mike waved angrily toward the cultivated fields. "*That* is what's the matter!" he burst out. "We come out here to fight drug traffickers, and all we do is take a few pictures . . . maybe take the local boys on a few mock raids. In the meantime, these people keep on growing coca as though we were never here.

"And where's it all going? There's a cocaine ring buying it up and turning it into poison—while *we take pictures!*"

"But isn't that why you're here?" Jenny asked in confusion. "To find that cocaine ring and arrest them?"

"*Find* them? There are thousands of square miles of jungle down there—and a dozen hiding places in each mile! It would take a miracle to find them. And if we *do,* they'll just bribe a few local officials and be back at it in no time."

Mike gave a short laugh, but his angry eyes showed no humor. "You don't know how powerful these guys are. In fairy tales the good guys triumph, but in real life, the bad guys are definitely winning."

The twins were stunned at his outburst, but Jenny leaned over and touched Mike on the arm. "Please don't feel so bad, Mike. God will punish them in the end."

The black eyes blazed with anger. "God? You wouldn't believe that Sunday school garbage if you'd grown up in a black slum like I did—ten people in a three-room apartment, toilets that didn't work, cockroaches . . ."

He glanced down at the wide-eyed children, then added, ". . . and a lot of other things you don't need to know. The army got me out of there, but my sister wasn't so lucky. You tell me what kind of God lets a fifteen-year-old girl die of a cocaine overdose . . . while the man who sold her the stuff walks off scot-free. I'd rather not believe in God than think He's letting creeps like that live!"

Justin shook his head in frustration. "Maybe Uncle Pete could explain it to you," he said.

Mike's soft drawl was loaded with scorn: "Sure, pass the buck! I figured you didn't have any real answers!"

Troubled, Justin said slowly, "Well, I don't know why those things happen, but I do know God didn't make us robots. He lets us choose what we do. It isn't His fault so many people decide to do bad things."

He thought back on the last few days and added, "But I've learned one thing lately; God is more powerful than any cocaine smugglers, and He *will* punish them in the end."

"We're really sorry about your sister," Jenny added gently. "I wish there was something we could do to help."

"There is!" Justin answered, remembering those long hours in the Cave of the Inca Re. "We can pray. We'll pray that you find that cocaine ring. Right, Jenny?"

"Sure, you do that," Mike answered sarcastically. No one said another word during the remaining minutes of their flight back to base.

An hour later, Special Agent Turner and Mike were bent over the developed photos from the flight. Justin and Jenny stretched their necks to see over the men's shoulders. Straightening up, the DEA agent clapped Mike on the shoulder. "Great job, Mike! Those close-ups are excellent. Some of them look like they were shot almost at ground level."

Justin glanced up to see a momentary look of embarrassment on Mike's face. Mike shrugged, and Justin looked down. Special Agent Turner moved away from the broad worktable where the prints were spread out. His hands in the pockets of his khaki-colored canvas trousers, he grinned at the impatiently waiting children.

"So, you kids want to check out what you've been doing this afternoon. Go ahead, take a look!"

Justin eagerly bent over the table. Most of the shots showed nothing but an unchanging view of the unbroken mass of jungle. Then he came to the pictures of the coca field. He could see the long green rows of coca plants, divided by protective ridges of earth. At one end a huge tangle of vegetation concealed a vehicle that might be a jeep or perhaps a small pickup. In another picture, a tiny figure stared upward, one hand shielding his eyes from the sun. A large hay rake lay abandoned on the green pile beside him.

"Hey, look at this one!" Jenny exclaimed, thrusting an enlarged photo under his nose. "You can practically see their faces."

The aerial camera must have still been running when Mike buzzed the hut, because the picture showed a close-up view of three dark-haired men standing in the doorway of the hut. Two of them stared up at the helicopter, mouths open with surprise. The third man had thrown an arm across his face and was frozen in the act of ducking into the hut.

Justin studied the third man closely. His close-cropped hair was dark but grizzled with gray, and he looked as though he would be tall if standing straight. It was impossible to distinguish facial features, but something seemed familiar about the pointed chin and the set of broad shoulders.

Jenny put another print into his hands. This one showed three men diving away from the helicopter into the jungle. He took a closer look. From the helicopter window he had counted three men scurrying toward the cover of the trees. Now he noticed that one of the running men wore the same ragged clothing as the worker who had been raking coca leaves in the first picture.

Jenny pointed to a dark figure hidden within the shadow of the doorway. "That's the only one who didn't come out in the open," she commented. "It's like he knew we were taking pictures."

Justin glanced back and forth between the two prints. Suddenly he remembered a similar dark figure standing at the edge of the oil camp the night before, his sharp features shaded in just the same manner.

He shook his head, then looked again. It was a crazy idea, but he could have sworn that the third man in those pictures was the chief geologist of the oil camp, Dr. Latour!

Chapter Four

A SUSPICIOUS CONVERSATION

JUSTIN AWOKE with a start the next morning. The first rays of the sun, filtered through the mosquito net, made a pattern of diamonds across the camp bed. He sat up suddenly. Something was wrong.

A high-pitched scream rang out again. "Uncle Pete! Justin! Oh, help! There's something horrible in here!"

Justin threw off the thin sheet that covered him. Without waiting to put on shoes, he rushed across the room. Uncle Pete was close behind him as he crashed open the door to the other room.

Jenny stood on top of a small metal dresser that looked as though it had been converted from an old filing cabinet. Dancing from one bare foot to the other, she pointed to the floor. She tried to speak, but only a squeak came out. She swallowed and tried again. *"Th-There!* It's just *horrible!"*

Justin followed the direction of her shaking finger. On the floor, just crawling out of one of Jenny's shoes, was an insect about three inches long. It crouched on eight legs; a pair of claws extended out in front like those of a miniature crab. A wicked-looking, bony tail as long as its body lashed back and forth.

As Justin bent to look closer, Uncle Pete blocked his way with one arm. "Don't get too close, Justin. That thing packs quite a sting in its tail."

Grabbing a hairbrush from where it had been dropped on the floor, he whacked repeatedly at the strange insect. When it lay motionless on the cement floor, Uncle Pete lifted Jenny down. "Okay, what happened?"

Jenny gulped. "I was getting dressed, and I picked up my Adidas to put them on, and . . . and I saw *that!*"

Picking up the hairbrush, Justin flicked the insect over. "I've never seen anything like this before," he said with interest. "I wonder if it's poisonous?"

Uncle Pete looked grim. "That's a scorpion. And, yes, they can be very poisonous. Now you know why Alan told you to shake out your shoes and clothes before putting them on."

"Well, I'll sure never forget again!" Jenny assured him.

Justin was careful to shake out his own clothes, and ten minutes later, the three Parkers joined Alan on his veranda for breakfast. After breakfast, Uncle Pete told the twins they would have to keep themselves occupied again as he and Alan would be busy most of the day.

"Alan, I'd like to run a few tests of my own. Could you turn on one of the pumps this morning?"

Alan looked surprised. "Sure. But why? Is there a problem with Dr. Latour's test results?"

"It doesn't hurt to double-check," Uncle Pete answered vaguely.

Justin groaned inwardly at the thought of another long day sitting around camp. Catching his disappointed look, Uncle Pete added, "I know this trip hasn't been too exciting for you kids so far, but I haven't forgotten my promise to take you into the jungle. Before we left La Paz, Mr. Evans arranged for us to visit some friends of his. Our guide should be arriving tomorrow."

The prospect of a trip into the jungle kept Jenny and Justin chattering like monkeys for much of the morning. Stretched out on a pair of worn-out lawn chairs, they talked about what they might see—neither having much idea of what the jungle was like.

But by about ten, they were bored again. Following Uncle Pete and Alan out to the oil field, they watched them gather samples of the black crude oil.

After lunch, the two men disappeared into the camp office. Jenny buried her nose in the pile of dusty magazines that Alan had found somewhere, while Justin whittled on a dry branch with a sharp pocketknife.

A sudden dig of the knife snapped the limb in two. Justin jumped to his feet and announced, "I think I'll head over to the DEA camp. I want to take another look at those pictures."

Jenny dropped her magazine. "Me, too! I'll go crazy if I sit around here much longer."

When the twins wandered into the DEA encampment, this time the guards merely glanced at them and went about their duties. Justin and Jenny paused in the open doorway of the office. Half-hidden behind a screen, Special Agent Turner bent over a computer console. Mike stood over a table, shuffling through a pile of reports.

The sudden shadow across the doorway caught the DEA agent's attention, and he swung his office chair around to face the door. Regarding his visitors through alert gray eyes, he boomed, "Well, what are you waiting for? Come on in!"

As Justin and Jenny stepped into the main work area, the DEA agent demanded warmly, "Okay, you didn't come just to pay a social visit. What is it you want?"

Justin asked hesitantly, "Uh, we were wondering if we could look at those pictures again. You know, the ones Mike took yesterday?"

Special Agent Turner waved them across the room. "Go ahead and look. They're still on the table there. Just don't touch anything else. Turn on that overhead lamp if you need more light."

Justin quickly found the pictures he had studied the day before. Holding them up to the light, he examined them closely. He searched through the rest of the prints, looking for other close-ups of the clearing. Yes, there was another shot of the third man hiding in the doorway of the hut. Once again, his features were indistinct, but the profile looked familiar.

He held out the prints to his sister. "Does this guy remind you of anyone?"

Jenny glanced at the pictures and shook her head. "Not really."

"Come on! You didn't even look!"

Jenny shrugged. "What difference does it make! Who would we know out here, anyway?"

Justin ignored the question as he bent over the pictures again. No, he must be mistaken. After all, there were a lot of tall, dark-haired men in the world. Still! He held the last picture up to the light.

Jenny picked up another print that showed the carefully spaced rows of coca plants. "Uhh . . . Mr. Turner, why do the farmers grow this stuff? I mean, can't the government tell them to plant something else? Then you wouldn't have to worry about cocaine anymore."

Mike looked up from the stack of reports he was reading. "It isn't that easy!" he answered bitterly. "There's no law against growing coca, and who's going to stop growing it when you can make ten times as much money as with any other crop?"

Special Agent Turner swung his chair around to face the two children. "That's right. The cocaine dealers have made coca a high-paying crop. And with so much money to be made these days, more and more land is being cleared for coca growing. Fifteen years ago, Bolivia grew only 30,000 acres of coca—mainly in the Chaparé, the southeastern corner of Bolivia—just enough for their traditional chewing. Now, 150,000 more acres have been slashed out of jungle areas to produce cocaine—thousands of acres out of this part of the Beni. It's illegal to open up new coca cultivations, but that law is rarely enforced."

"But don't they care about all the crimes and people who get killed from cocaine use?" Jenny asked in disbelief.

"Jenny, most of these growers are just dirt-poor peasants who see coca as the best way of providing for their family. All they know is that their children can grow strong and healthy on good food if they grow coca. And there is money for school, where once their kids could never have had an education. Few have ever seen what cocaine does."

Special Agent Turner leaned back in his chair and waved a pencil. "You've got to remember that Bolivia is very poor. The only thing keeping the country going is money from coca. The U.S. and other wealthy countries are sponsoring programs to grow soybeans and other crops instead of coca, but they aren't working very well."

Justin was thinking hard. "What about the ones who buy the leaves? Couldn't you find out who's buying up the leaves and arrest them?"

Mike laughed harshly. "Anyone who wants to can buy coca leaves. You'd have to prove it was being turned into cocaine. Besides, we can't arrest anyone!"

"Mike is right, Justin," the gray-haired DEA agent stated. "The U.S. and Bolivian governments made a deal to bring us here, but we really don't have any authority. We teach their soldiers how to track down cocaine labs. And we gather evidence against drug traffickers. But only the Bolivian narcotics force, the UMOPAR, can arrest them—and even *they* are under orders from government officials."

"And there are plenty of them who wouldn't arrest a drug trafficker if we dropped one in their living room!" Mike added angrily. "Why, we know one man who has made millions from drugs. He's got a fabulous estate and a private airfield. The locals call him the 'Cocaine King.'"

"But why doesn't someone just arrest him?" Justin demanded.

"Because the police know that anyone who arrests him would be out of a job tomorrow," Mike answered grimly. "He has a lot of friends in high places and plenty of money to pay out in bribes."

"The president and many government officials are beginning to see the problems that cocaine brings," Special Agent Turner added. "They back us and the UMOPAR force all the way. But there are others who are only interested in getting their share of the cocaine money—and they have a lot of influence. They would use any excuse to kick us out of the country. So we can't do much unless we actually catch traffickers in the act."

Justin waved an arm around the room. "Why do you even bother trying to help, then? Why don't you just stay home?"

"Because cocaine and drug smuggling isn't just our country's problem," the DEA agent answered seriously. "It hurts people all over the world. And it won't be stamped out until countries and people start working together."

Looking at Justin and Jenny's unhappy faces, he suddenly smiled. "It isn't all bad. If we track down a cache of cocaine, we have the authority to destroy it."

Jenny latched on to an unfamiliar word. "Catch? You mean, like 'catch the ball'?"

Special Agent Turner smiled. "No, a *cache* . . . a secret stash."

Somewhere out there is a cocaine lab producing hundreds of pounds of the drug. If we can find out how the cocaine is leaving the country, we can arrest the smugglers on the other end."

Justin was still shuffling through the aerial photographs. Suddenly he exclaimed, "Hey, look at this clearing! Maybe it's that lab you've been looking for."

Carrying a photo of thick jungle over to Special Agent Turner, he excitedly pointed out a bare spot among the trees. Glancing at the picture, the DEA agent laughed. "Sorry, Justin. If we checked out every open space in the jungle, we'd never get this job done. That's probably some poor farmer's field, or even a natural clearing."

He patted him on the shoulder. "You've got a good eye, though, so I'll tell you what we're looking for. When you find an open strip in those aerials long enough to land a small plane, there's a good chance you'll find a lab nearby."

"There wasn't anything like that in the pictures," Justin said with disappointment. "Maybe the cocaine lab is somewhere else."

Mike whirled around. "Who do you think is buying up all that coca we saw? No, they're out there. We've just got to find them."

Moving over to the open door, he stared out toward the line of jungle that bordered the camp, his broad face full of anger. "If I had my way, we wouldn't just be sitting here taking pictures. I'd blast every coca field out of existence—along with the creeps who peddle that poison!"

His hands at his sides in hard fists, Mike hurried out the door.

Special Agent Turner sighed as he looked after him. "Don't mind Mike. He takes this job very seriously."

Jenny nodded. "Yeah, he told us about his sister."

Special Agent Turner went on. "Mike was just out of high school when that happened. He joined up with the Drug Enforcement Agency shortly afterward. He's turned his job into a personal war against drug traffickers."

Justin returned the photo to the table. "Well, I guess we'd better be going. Thanks for your time, sir. It's been very interesting." Jenny followed him toward the door.

"Any time!" Special Agent Turner walked them across the cut lawn that surrounded the base. "I wish every kid knew a few facts about cocaine. We'd have a lot less work to do."

At the edge of the encampment, Justin suddenly stopped. "Sir, do you know Dr. Latour very well? You know . . . the chief geologist at the oil camp?"

"We checked out all the camp personnel before we came down," Special Agent Turner answered. "He has an excellent record and, I understand, a lot of friends in high places in the government. But I've never met him. He hasn't been around here since we arrived."

His keen eyes suddenly sharpened with interest. "Why do you ask?"

"Oh, I was just wondering," Justin answered hastily. "Thanks!"

The sun was setting in the short twilight of the tropics by the time the twins set off for the oil camp. Jenny broke into Justin's thoughts.

"I sure learned a lot today. Poor Mike! I wish he wasn't so angry all the time, but I can't blame him for hating drug dealers."

"Well, there isn't much we can do about him or the drug dealers . . . except pray, like we promised," Justin answered.

"Why don't we pray right now?" Jenny suggested. The twins stopped where they were and bowed their heads.

The instant night of the tropics had fallen by the time Justin and Jenny drew near to the lights of the oil camp buildings. The narrow path, lit only by the hard glitter of countless stars, led along the back side of the lab. Justin had just passed under the window that had stood open their first night—it was now shut tight—when he suddenly put out an arm.

"Shh! Listen!" he hissed.

A faint gleam shone from a triangular-shaped break in the shutter just above them. Jenny stopped, staring at Justin in surprise. Over the stillness, angry voices rose from inside the lab. Jenny pushed past her brother. Standing on tiptoe, she peered through the small hole.

"It's just Dr. Latour and Rodrigo, back from their trip," she whispered loudly.

Justin quickly pressed a hand against her mouth as he placed his own eye to the opening. He could see only a small section of the long, narrow lab, but he saw Dr. Latour's assistant leaning against the counter across the room.

"This has really loused things up badly!" Dr. Latour paced into Justin's sight, blocking off his view of the room. His back was to the window, but Justin could tell he was very angry.

"Why didn't I know about this DEA operation . . . or that Parker was coming? It was your job to keep a close eye on Green's communications."

"Don't go putting the blame on me! I wasn't even here at the time." Though Justin couldn't see him, a slight accent identified Rodrigo as the speaker. "If you had reported in last week, we wouldn't have this problem."

"You know that was impossible," Dr. Latour answered coldly.

"And it was those tests you sent in that brought Parker down. Now he's even talking about closing down the camp. Our whole operation is in jeopardy!"

Dr. Latour suddenly moved toward the counter that ran along the back wall of the lab. Justin ducked as the geologist paused just inside the window. "It doesn't matter now," he said clearly, in calmer tones. "This is our last haul anyway. We'll be done in a week."

"But the DEA is swarming all over the place!" Rodrigo grumbled.

"Don't worry about the DEA." Dr. Latour moved away from the window, and Justin inched up to peer in again. "They aren't interested in us. It's Parker and those kids I'm concerned about. I don't like them prowling around the place. See to it they stay off my back until it's all over."

The two men moved out of sight, and Justin heard the heavy metal door of the lab swing open. "Don't you worry!" Rodrigo's slight accent floated back. "It's all taken care of."

His gloomy words changed to triumph. "I've got just the person to deal with them! And if that doesn't work, there are other ways to get them out of camp!"

Chapter Five

STRANGER IN BLACK

"RISE AND shine!" Justin opened his bleary eyes. In the faint predawn light, he could barely make out Uncle Pete standing beside his bed. When he didn't move, Uncle Pete grabbed the edge of the camp bed and tipped Justin onto the hard concrete floor.

"Let's go, Justin! We're leaving in less than an hour—with or without you."

Uncle Pete tossed a small canvas backpack onto the floor beside him. "You and Jenny can take anything that will fit in there. Just remember, you'll have to carry it!"

Justin was instantly wide awake as he realized this was the day of the promised jungle trip. He hurriedly pulled on his clothes and shoved spare underwear, T-shirts, and an extra pair of jeans into the backpack. Then he added a small, leather-bound Bible.

"Here's my stuff," Jenny said, dumping a pile of clothing on the bed.

"Hey, you can't take all that!" Justin protested. "We're going to the jungle, not a party!"

Ruthlessly sorting through the pile, he shoved back half the clothes. Jenny reluctantly began folding the remainder.

Justin checked through his camera case and added several more rolls of film. This reminded him of their visit to the DEA base the day before.

"Hey, Jenny," he asked, "are you sure you didn't recognize anyone in those pictures yesterday?"

Jenny shoved her clothes into the backpack. "Yes, of course I'm sure. Why? Did you?"

Justin ran a hand through his hair, making it stand straight up. "I could have sworn one of those guys in the hut was Dr. Latour."

"Don't be silly!" Jenny answered scornfully. "What would *he* be doing there?"

"Well, you heard what he said last night. Maybe he's mixed up in that business Mr. Turner is looking into."

"Yes, I heard what he said. He's worried about Uncle Pete shutting down the camp, and he wants us out of here. So what? He's probably afraid he might lose his job."

She headed toward the door. "You heard what Mr. Turner said. They've checked out everyone in the oil camp. Besides, why shouldn't he be out there? Alan said he was doing surveys in the jungle. Maybe he's found oil near there."

Justin was half-convinced. Maybe his suspicions *were* silly. After all, wanting visitors to clear out didn't make a man a criminal. His dad was the same way when *he* was working on some big project. Besides, it was none of their business.

Pink barely stained the eastern sky as Justin and Jenny joined Uncle Pete for a quick breakfast. Alan was nowhere in sight, but seated beside Uncle Pete was a slim man of medium height who had the thin, dark features and curly hair common to people of the Beni-Brazil border area.

"This is Eduardo," Uncle Pete introduced. "At least I think it is. I couldn't understand much of what he said, but he mentioned Mr. Evans's name, so I assume he is our guide."

Justin glanced around. "Where is everyone else?"

"Dr. Latour and Rodrigo aren't up yet," Uncle Pete answered. "Alan is refueling the camp helicopter. He will drop us off at the river Mamoré, where we'll catch a boat."

He was interrupted by the loud drone of an approaching aircraft. Moments later, the small helicopter the twins had seen the day they arrived settled onto the gravel driveway. Alan jumped down as the rotor blades slowed to a stop.

"There's no rush," he grinned as Justin and Jenny looked with dismay at their untouched breakfast. "I could use another cup of coffee myself."

"Maybe you could help us out while you're here," Uncle Pete interjected. "I've picked up a bit of Spanish in my travels, but not enough to understand Eduardo here."

He gestured toward their silent visitor. "I'd like to know a bit about him and our destination before we end up in the middle of the jungle without a translator."

Alan turned to the man. At the sound of his strongly accented Spanish, the solemn, dark face brightened into a wide smile. Justin strained to listen, but he couldn't understand a single word.

"His name is Eduardo Villaroel," Alan translated, turning back to the three Americans, "and he is taking you to his village far up the Mamoré River. He is very glad to meet friends of Mr. Evans."

"How did he meet Mr. Evans clear out here?" Jenny asked. Alan repeated the question.

"I, like all my family, was a grower of the coca," Alan translated. The twins looked at each other in startled surprise.

"Mr. Evans came to our village many months ago," Alan continued. "He told us things we had never heard before about the Son of God, Jesus Christ—about how He loved all men and had given up His own life to pay for the sins of men. He told us how Jesus Christ had come to life again and has the power to change our lives, if we will follow Him. I knew in my heart that this *gringo* spoke the truth. My wife and I made up our minds to follow this Jesus."

Alan knit his eyebrows together as he tried to put Eduardo's exact words into English. "After Mr. Evans left, we began to walk long distances to hear more of Jesus. One day, Mr. Evans came and took me to Santa Cruz to learn from God's Word with many other followers of Jesus.

"It was there that I learned of the evil of the cocaine—the white powder made from our coca leaves. I saw even young children dying from taking this powder. I thought of my *guagua*, my little girl."

He made a motion of cradling a baby. "What if someday *she* learned to do this evil? I decided to stop growing coca."

Eduardo broke into another flood of Spanish. "Mr. Evans came and helped us to plant soya and food for my family instead. Now others of my family have also decided to follow Jesus and have left the coca. We have even built a church."

Eduardo stood up, motioning excitedly with his hands. "Come with me! I will show you my village and my family and the church we have built."

As Alan finished translating, Eduardo marched down the veranda steps, ready to leave immediately. Uncle Pete chuckled. "I guess we'd better go before we get left behind."

The twins had been listening intently, but now hurriedly swallowed the last of their breakfast and followed the three men to the helicopter. They had just buckled their seatbelts when Dr. Latour and Rodrigo came down the steps of the bungalow next to Alan's.

"Just a minute!" Uncle Pete said, tapping Alan on the shoulder. Leaning out, he called, "Dr. Latour! Could I have a word with you?"

Dr. Latour strolled over to the helicopter. "Leaving, eh?" he said pleasantly.

"Just overnight," Uncle Pete replied. "I've finished going through your reports. I found some of your surveys very interesting. When we get home tomorrow, I'd like to fly out and investigate the sites for myself."

Dr. Latour looked displeased. "Don't you trust my work?"

"I'm sure your work is of the highest quality," Uncle Pete answered flatly, "but my job requires that I check things out for myself."

Dr. Latour nodded abruptly. "Of course! I'll be available when you're ready."

He was turning away when Jenny leaned forward. "By the way, Dr. Latour, we saw a picture of you yesterday. I mean Justin did . . . I mean, he *thinks* he did."

Startled, Dr. Latour turned around. "What do you mean, girl?"

"When we were flying with Mike, the DEA pilot, yesterday,"

Jenny explained chattily. "He took pictures from the helicopter. It *was* you, wasn't it?"

Dr. Latour looked displeased. "It's possible, I suppose. We did hear a helicopter fly over at one of the survey sites. Now, if you'll excuse me . . ."

"A helicopter *just flew over?*" Justin whispered fiercely to Jenny as the camp copter lifted off. "Why did you bring that up, anyway?"

"You said you wanted to know!" Jenny answered reasonably. "Now that the mystery's solved, let's enjoy the trip."

Jenny was right, Justin had to admit. He had looked forward to this trip too long to let anything spoil it. He turned his attention to the window. In less than an hour, a broad river spread out beneath them. Sitting behind the pilot's seat, Justin exclaimed, "Wow, look at all those boats! I thought hardly anyone lived here."

Below the rapidly descending helicopter, hundreds of strangely assorted boats plowed a passage up and down the waterway. Their wake stained the rocky shoreline a muddy brown. A few dilapidated piers, extending far out over the beach, indicated how high the river would rise in rainy season.

"You'll find a lot more boats in the Beni than cars," Alan answered as he landed gently on the beach. "There aren't many roads out here, and the rivers are the lifelines between villages and towns."

The helicopter had landed only yards away from the river's edge. The party of four climbed out. As Uncle Pete gave Alan final instructions, Justin reached for the backpacks. He lifted Uncle Pete's, grunting in surprise. Justin was a husky boy, but he was puffing as he lowered the pack to the ground.

As Alan took off, spraying his passengers with sand, Justin demanded, "What in the world do you have in there, Uncle Pete?"

"Oh, just the UHF radio and a few odds and ends." Uncle Pete shouldered the pack with ease. "Oh, and a car battery, of course, to power the radio."

Justin eyed Uncle Pete with new respect as he shouldered his own lighter pack. Eduardo hadn't said anything since they left camp, but now he mumbled something to Uncle Pete. Justin caught the word *barco*. Uncle Pete pulled out a pocket Spanish-English dictionary and leafed through it.

"*Barco* means boat," Uncle Pete said at last. As Eduardo nodded and pointed down the beach, he added, "I think we're supposed to follow him."

The three Parkers followed Eduardo along the waterfront to where a funny-looking boat bobbed beside the pier. Its deck was wide and flat like a cargo barge, its low railing only a few feet above water level.

In the center, a ramshackle structure of scrap lumber and tin rose two stories above the deck. Rusty barrels, boxes and bags, and even livestock, crowded the deck. A steady stream of passengers was making its way up the wide wooden plank that connected the boat to shore.

"Look!" Jenny pointed. "That must be how they drive the boat!"

"*Steer* the boat!" Justin corrected, his gaze following her finger. On the second story, a small, rail-lined deck protruded in front of a tiny cabin. Above the rail was a large, spoked wheel. A man in a faded blue uniform leaned calmly against the wheel, a battered seaman's cap slanted over one eye. Catching sight of the two young Americans, he straightened up and waved in their direction. Jenny waved back.

Uncle Pete was already following their guide up the gangplank. Justin pushed his sister along in the direction of the boat. At that moment, the passenger in front of them stumbled, dropping a heavy burlap bag. Justin stopped so suddenly that he lost his balance, bumping into the person behind him.

Catching himself, Justin turned to apologize, then opened his eyes wide in surprise. Dressed in new jeans and cowboy-style shirt, the man behind him was so thin that his skin seemed to be stretched tight over bare bones. In spite of the heat, a black leather jacket hung loosely from skeletal shoulders. What could be seen of his face behind a pair of oversize sunglasses had an unusual yellow tint.

"I'm sorry!" Justin stammered, stepping backward. The man slowly lifted his sunglasses, and strangely unfocused eyes, rimmed with red, stared back at the twins. Without a word, the man turned and disappeared into the crowd.

Justin stared after him until he heard a familiar voice calling, "Justin! Jenny!" It was Uncle Pete, leaning over the rail of the boat. A foghorn bellowed, and he realized that the gangplank was being pulled away from the shore.

"Wait for us!" Justin grabbed his sister's hand and ran for the boat.

Joining the others at the rail, Justin and Jenny watched the boat putt putt slowly away from the bank. Just yards away, an oversize canoe slid by, propelled by an outboard motor. It was so heavily loaded with people and goods that the wooden sides rose only inches above the water level.

"Hey, there's people *living* on that one!" Justin pointed out a smaller, one story version of their own boat. A woman stood on the deck, hanging wet clothing on a rope stretched from the cabin to the rail. A toddler played in the middle of barrels and boxes, a rope around his waist keeping him from falling into the water.

A shrill whistle turned their attention upward. The boat pilot leaned down from above, grinning broadly. Casually turning the big wheel with one hand, he motioned for them to come up with the other.

Justin glanced toward Uncle Pete. Deep in conversation with Eduardo, he was shuffling through the Spanish-English dictionary to find words to supplement his meager Spanish vocabulary.

"Come on!" he urged his sister. "I've always wanted to meet a real riverboat pilot."

The two quickly climbed up the steep ladder that led to the second-story deck. The pilot, his seaman's cap smartly pushed to one side, greeted them with a grin and a flow of Spanish.

When Justin and Jenny shook their heads regretfully, he resorted to sign language. Waving around at the boat, he pointed to himself. *"Capitán!"* he repeated.

"I think that means he is the captain of the boat," Justin said. He pointed to the pilot and asked loudly, "Captain?"

The man nodded. *"Sí! Sí! Capitán!"* Waving his graceful dark hands, he indicated that Justin should take the wheel.

"Me? Steer the boat?" Justin carefully took the wheel with both hands. A stiff breeze cooled his freckled face as he watched the river flow slowly past the sides of the boat.

"Wow! This is great!" he exclaimed, turning the wheel as he had seen the captain do.

"No! No!" The riverboat captain snatched the wheel from Justin's hands. Looking down, Justin saw that the boat was drifting close to the shore. The captain yanked the wheel, and the prow of the boat slowly moved away from shore.

This done, the captain grinned, his good humor restored. But he didn't offer them the wheel again. Justin watched the captain effortlessly rotate the wheel back and forth, keeping the boat on a straight course upriver.

"There's more to steering this thing than I thought," he said gloomily.

The twins moved over to the railing. They were out of sight of the small river town now, and thick jungle pressed down to the river's edge. Jenny scanned the deck below, searching for Uncle Pete and Eduardo. Suddenly she stiffened, and poked her brother in the ribs. "Hey, isn't that the guy we bumped into on the beach?"

Justin looked down. Leaning against the rail was a skeletally thin man in a black leather jacket. As though he felt their gaze, the man looked up. He stared at the two for a moment, then turned and disappeared around the side of the cabin.

Jenny shuddered. "That guy gives me the creeps!"

"I wonder how he got on the boat," Justin answered thoughtfully. "He was heading in the opposite direction when we saw him, and we were at the end of the line. He must have circled around and cut in front of us."

Jenny suddenly lost interest in the man. "Hey, take a look at that!" She scrambled down the ladder. Hurriedly thanking the captain, Justin followed her to the bow of the boat.

The river was narrower here, and the boat passed close to the shore. A rotting log as thick as a man was tall extended down to the river.

"What's the big deal?" Justin grumbled. "It's just an old log!"

"Not the *log!*" Jenny answered impatiently "Look what's *on* the log!"

Justin looked more closely. What looked like one of the heavy vines that covered the jungle trees was draped across the log, it was about eight inches thick. Then he saw the vine move.

"It's a boa constrictor!" he exclaimed. "And what a big one!"

The giant snake slowly slithered its way down into the underbrush. Justin and Jenny watched as more and more of its length moved up over the log and down the other side. The tail came into view just as the log fell behind the boat.

Justin lowered his camera in awe. "It must have been thirty feet long!"

Uncle Pete moved up beside them. "They get bigger than that north of here. A friend of mine once told me an amazing story. He was working with the Indians on a jungle river up north. A gigantic tree had fallen into the water there. He says he watched a snake a full yard thick come up out of the water and over that log. He got out of there pretty quick, so he never did get to measure the thing, but he figures it must have been at least a hundred feet long."

"Do you think it was a true story?" Justin asked doubtfully.

Uncle Pete's green eyes crinkled with a smile. "Yes, I believe it. You see, he had a photo with him. It showed an Indian guide standing on the bank with that snake sliding over the log behind them. There must have been a good forty feet of the snake showing above water."

His explanation was interrupted by a squeal from Jenny.

Justin drew in his breath sharply as he followed the direction of her gaze. A patch of white, sandy beach lay between the river and the jungle. Stretched out lazily on the warm sand was a catlike animal the size of a large dog. Odd-shaped black circles dotted its short, golden fur, and its short tail twitched, apparently from a bad dream.

"Is that a real tiger?"

"Of course not, it's a jaguar!" Justin told his sister. "Isn't it, Uncle Pete?"

"Well, it looks just like a big kitten!" Jenny answered. "I'd love to pet it."

"Don't kid yourself," Uncle Pete answered. "The jaguar is one of the most vicious fighters of the jungle. It'll even hunt down a man if it finds one alone and defenseless."

Justin watched the sleeping animal with more respect. "I think I'd just as soon keep the river in between us!"

As though aware of their conversation, the jaguar lazily turned gold-green eyes toward the intruders who had interrupted his nap. It gave a wide, bored yawn, the boat passing so close that Justin could see the pink of its long tongue.

The twins watched breathlessly as the graceful animal stretched, its muscles rippling under the sleek pelt. Without looking back at its spellbound audience, it stalked leisurely into the tangle of trees. Justin sighed with pleasure. Now *this* was his idea of jungle!

Shortly after noon, the riverboat docked at a small landing on the edge of the jungle; it actually was nothing more than a cluster of thatched huts along a strip of muddy shore. Justin half-slid down the steep wooden plank onto the shore. Jenny and the others followed.

"Is this where we're staying?" Jenny waved around at the handful of huts. But Eduardo said something and was motioning toward the thick, unbroken trees behind the tiny village. He held up two fingers.

"We have to walk for two hours," Uncle Pete told the twins after consulting his dictionary again.

Jenny looked at the mass of green. "Through that?"

"Of course!" Uncle Pete answered sternly, but his eyes crinkled with amusement at her worried expression. "You said you wanted to see the jungle!"

Justin and Uncle Pete adjusted their backpacks, and the Parkers followed Eduardo up a narrow path that pierced the jungle. Fresh hoof marks showed that it was well-traveled. Tall hardwoods, covered with vines and orchids, shut out the sun but locked in the steamy heat. Eduardo swung a machete at undergrowth that threatened to overrun the path.

Shifting his backpack to a more comfortable position, Justin wiped beads of sweat from his face and wished that he had brought mosquito repellent. The air was noisy with the chatter of birds and the "ooh, ooh" of the small brown monkeys that lived in the tall trees. One tiny, wrinkled face peered out curiously from under fan-shaped, green leaves before a hairy arm reached out to snatch the infant away.

Several times as they hiked along, Justin heard crackling in the underbrush along the path. *More wild animals,* he thought with satisfaction. An hour into their hike, Uncle Pete called for a rest break and uncapped a canteen of boiled water. As Justin tipped up the canteen, he again heard the snap of a branch close behind. Jenny grabbed his arm.

"Look! Someone's following us!"

Justin whirled around. A dozen yards behind them, a man had stumbled into the path. The man ducked behind a tree. Justin dropped his backpack and ran back down the path. The man had disappeared by the time Justin reached the spot where he had stood, but not before Justin recognized a now-familiar black leather jacket.

Chapter Six

FIRE!

JENNY HURRIED to catch up as Justin stared into the gloomy tangle of trees. "That was the man we saw earlier, wasn't it?" she panted. "I *know* he's following us."

"What are you talking about, Jenny?" Uncle Pete asked as they rejoined the others. "What man?"

Justin explained about the man they had seen on the dock and later in the boat. "He really *was* watching us," he concluded.

Uncle Pete turned to Eduardo and again pulled out his Spanish-English dictionary. But Eduardo only shook his head at Uncle Pete's halting questions.

"We sure could use a translator *now!*" Uncle Pete said with exasperation. "At any rate, Eduardo didn't see the man and doesn't know who it could be."

"Well, he sure looked creepy!" Jenny said with a shiver.

"I think you kids are making too much out of this," Uncle Pete answered firmly. "He was probably a local on his way home to his village."

"Then why was he staring at us . . . and sneaking around in the bush like that?" Jenny questioned.

"Maybe he's never seen foreigners before." Uncle Pete

dismissed the subject. "Anyway, if we're going to get anywhere today, we'd better get moving."

Justin and Jenny exchanged an unconvinced glance, but began walking. An hour later, a good-sized town spread out in front of them. Thatched houses, with a few brick buildings mixed in, lined broad, muddy streets. There were even a few storefronts and a tiny central plaza.

A road divided the village in half. Though it was unpaved and rutted, it was at least as good as the road that led to the oil camp. Beyond the wide-spaced buildings, the twins glimpsed what looked suspiciously like a grass-strip runway.

"Welcome to Magdalena," Uncle Pete boomed with a broad smile.

Hands on her hips, Jenny looked up irritably at her uncle. "And you made us walk all this way? We could have flown into here!"

Uncle Pete's eyes were playful. "You *did* say you wanted to see the jungle!"

Jenny's indignant glare relaxed into a grin. "Yeah, I guess I did."

"At any rate, you'll get your chance to fly tomorrow." Uncle Pete tapped the backpack he carried. "That's why I brought the UHF radio along. When we're ready to go, I'll give Alan a call and he'll fly in to pick us up."

"Tomorrow?" she asked in dismay. "So soon?"

"That's right! I have a job to do back at the oil camp, remember?" A frown wrinkled Uncle Pete's forehead. "There's a few things I just don't understand. . . ."

Jenny looked puzzled, but Justin suddenly realized it was long past lunch time. Clutching his stomach dramatically, he moaned, "Do you realize we haven't eaten since breakfast? I'm starved!"

"What do you mean you haven't eaten?" Jenny answered. "What about all that junk you bought on the boat?"

She counted on her fingers. "Let's see, cheese rolls, and tamales, and those meat shish kebabs—"

"Those didn't count!" Justin interrupted hastily. "That wasn't a real meal. Besides, I'm a growing boy!"

Uncle Pete laughed. "Come on! Let's find something to eat before you collapse in the street."

A short time later, Justin dipped into a bowl of hot, thick soup. "This is great!"

"What's in it?" Jenny asked doubtfully, dipping into her own bowl. She picked something out of the stew—and dropped it. "Justin! What's this?"

Justin leaned over and lifted out a long, narrow piece of bone. Running along the top of the bone was a perfect set of oversized molars!

"Uncle Pete," he asked faintly, "what kind of soup did Eduardo say this is?"

Eduardo had obviously caught the drift of the twins' remarks. Justin was sure he detected a twinkle in the dark eyes as he motioned toward the soup and repeated, *"Es sopa de cabeza de vaca."*

Justin reached for Uncle Pete's dictionary. "Cow head soup!" he exclaimed, giving his own bowl another stir. He swallowed hard as a round, rubbery object floated to the top. "An eyeball!"

Jenny shuddered. "Well, you can have *my* piece of cow head!"

Justin and Jenny felt much better when the smoky odors in

the small kitchen behind the open air restaurant resulted in plates heaped high with rice, potatoes, and what looked like fried bananas but was actually plantain, a starchy cooking banana. A smiling waitress topped each plate with one of the thick steaks that sizzled on a homemade grill made of heavy wire stretched six inches above a vast bed of coals.

"This is more like it!" Justin exclaimed, digging into the mound of food.

Full at last, the twins followed the two men across the small plaza. Justin kept an eye out for the man who had been following them, but saw no sign of a black leather jacket. Eduardo turned down a muddy alley which ended in a grove of palm trees. Sheltered under their long leaves was another of the now-familiar thatched huts.

This was the first time Justin had seen one up close. He studied the construction with interest. Saplings had been stripped of leaves and cut into poles the height of a man. Thrust into the ground close together to form walls, they were bound together with jungle vines to help keep them upright. Gaps between the poles allowed every breeze to cool the hut.

Laid over a wooden frame, a thick layer of palm and banana leaves formed the roof and hung down over the edges of the walls to keep the frequent rains out. A mat of lightweight reeds hung over the narrow doorway.

Eduardo knocked sharply against the wooden door frame. An elderly woman, a still-black braid hanging to her waist, lifted the mat and peered out cautiously. After a few exchanged remarks, Eduardo disappeared into a field behind the hut.

He returned a few minutes later, leading a pair of humpbacked

Brahman cattle. Harnessing them to a two-wheeled cart parked under the palms, he waved the Parkers into the cart with the same air of pride with which Justin's father showed off his new Trooper SUV.

"So this is the family car!" Jenny giggled as she tumbled into the cart. "But where are we going? Isn't this Eduardo's village?"

Uncle Pete shook his head. "Alan mentioned that Eduardo owned fields out of town a ways."

Eduardo cracked a rawhide whip over the bullocks' longhorned heads, and the wooden cart jolted into slow motion. He turned into the rutted road they had seen coming into town, and soon Magdalena faded from sight.

Small fields, chopped out of the jungle, led off from both sides of the road. Huge, vine-covered trees pressed against the edges of the small clearings—determined to take over the moment the farmers turned their backs. Justin noticed row after row of the same coca plants they had seen from the air two days before.

Braced against the side of the cart, Justin lifted his hot face to catch a late afternoon breeze, and breathed in deeply the sweet, damp smell of tropical flowers. Suddenly he sat up straight.

"Something's burning!" he exclaimed. Peering over one high wooden wheel, he saw a haze rising above the trees some distance ahead. "It looks like a forest fire!"

"Maybe some farmer is burning off a field," Uncle Pete remarked, but Eduardo too had suddenly straightened up. He leaned forward, staring in the direction of the smoke haze. Then with a loud crack, he struck the bullocks with his rawhide whip.

The twins tightly gripped the sides of the cart as the bullocks broke into a shambling run. Uncle Pete grabbed for his backpack just before the radio smashed against the cart wall. Hunched tensely over the reins, Eduardo urged the animals to move faster.

Minutes later, Eduardo jerked the bullocks to a halt. He was out of the cart and running before anyone else could move. Justin stared with horror at the scene before him.

It could hardly be called a village—just a dozen thatched huts built close together, with cleared fields fanning away on all sides. It had been a pleasant area, with orange and lemon trees shading the simple homes, and groves of young banana plants bordering the fields. Judging by one field to the left with waist-high rows of healthy green plants, the ground was fertile.

But now there was nothing pleasant left. Blackened heaps now smoldered where there had once been thatched huts. Bursts of flame shot through the heavy, black smoke that cloaked the once green rows of soybeans, while banana plants lay smashed into the ground.

A group of dark-haired people milled about among the ruins, the wailing of children rising above the anguished cries of adults. Catching sight of the new arrivals, a young woman with a toddler on one hip broke away from the group and ran to meet Eduardo. Her waist-length, blue-black braids were scorched, and tears streamed down her pretty, dark face.

"This doesn't look like an accident," Uncle Pete said grimly, stepping down from the cart and swinging his backpack to the ground. "Look at that house over there!"

Justin suddenly noticed that one of the houses of the group remained untouched. It bordered the one green field that remained. Eduardo loosened his wife's clinging arms and walked over to the remaining hut. A moment later, a man who could have been Eduardo's brother stepped out.

The man leaned against the door frame, his arms crossed over his chest. Eduardo spoke angrily, waving his arms toward the ruin around him. The other man answered sharply, then stepped back into the hut and dropped the mat shut behind him.

"What's going on, Uncle Pete?" Jenny inquired anxiously. "Why isn't that man helping the others?"

"Yeah, and how did this fire start, anyway?" Justin answered, staring around in dismay.

"I don't know," Uncle Pete answered, still grim. "But we'd better do something to help. I'm calling Alan in."

He pulled the rectangular black box that was the radio from his backpack and set it on the back of the cart, then added a car battery. Hooking cables to the battery terminals, Uncle Pete quickly stretched out a length of wire and looped the antenna over a nearby branch. Moments later he was speaking into a small, handheld microphone.

Switching off the radio, he turned to the waiting children. "Alan should be here within the hour. Then we'll find out what's happened here. In the meantime, let's see what we can do to help."

He paused for a moment. "I'm really sorry about this, kids," he added. "This has put an end to your jungle trip."

"That doesn't matter!" Justin answered quickly. "I just feel sorry for all these people."

"Poor Eduardo!" Jenny exclaimed. "How awful to come back to this. And he was so proud of his farm and his church."

"What can we do, Uncle Pete?" Justin added. "We'd like to help, too."

Uncle Pete gave them an approving look, then pulled a first aid kit out of his spacious backpack. "Okay, then! Let's see if there are any injuries. Justin, you get Eduardo. Jenny, help me unpack this stuff."

Justin found Eduardo standing among the half-burnt timbers of a larger thatched building, his dark eyes sad. Red-orange tongues of fire still licked the blackened remains of what had once been simple wooden benches. Justin guessed that this was the church Eduardo had told them about. Catching sight of him, Eduardo greeted Justin with a determined smile and followed him over to the cart.

For the next hour, Uncle Pete dressed burns and treated scratches and grazes. Eduardo worked with Uncle Pete, urging those in need of treatment over to the makeshift first aid post Uncle Pete had set up at the back of the cart. Only one person had been seriously hurt—a young woman who had tried to reenter her burning hut. She had only slight burns, but a falling branch had cut a deep gash across her forehead.

Jenny cuddled the woman's newborn son while Justin helped cut bandages and spread burn ointment. Those who didn't need treatment poked through the embers, searching for the few items that had escaped the flames—a few battered tin pots and pans, a twisted spoon, a blackened spade.

Uncle Pete was bandaging the last patient when they heard the drone of an approaching aircraft. Justin looked up from the roll of gauze he was packing away to see the camp helicopter lower onto a flat spot in the road. The rotors blew dust across the cart, then Alan was running toward them.

"What in the world is going on here?" he exclaimed, staring around in amazement.

"We hope you'll tell us!" Uncle Pete answered. Alan turned

to Eduardo, who had just dumped a pair of blackened ax heads he had salvaged beside the cart. In answer to his question, Eduardo poured out a flood of words, motioning angrily toward the ruins of his home.

Alan flushed red with anger as he listened. He turned to Uncle Pete. "He says an armed band of men came earlier today. They herded all the people out, then poured gasoline over the buildings and across the fields. Then they set everything on fire. They told the villagers it was a warning from the *narcotraficantes*—the cocaine dealers."

"But what about *that* house?" Justin asked suddenly. "How come that house and field didn't get burned?"

Alan turned to question Eduardo again, then answered, "The man who owns those agreed to start growing coca again. That's why he wasn't burned out."

A slow anger had been building up inside Justin ever since they had arrived. Now, gazing at the small group of children huddled fearfully on an unburned patch of grass, and the adults poking through the blackened embers of their homes, he suddenly understood Mike's bitterness toward the traffickers who had destroyed so many lives.

Maybe it is none of my business, but I'm going to do anything I can to help stop them! he vowed silently.

"We can't leave these people here like this," Uncle Pete said, interrupting Justin's thoughts. "Alan, ask Eduardo if he'd like us to ferry them into town. Maybe they can find land elsewhere."

Eduardo listened carefully as Alan explained Uncle Pete's idea, then moved away to talk with the rest of the fire victims. Moments later he was back, a group of the others with him.

Alan translated his exact words as he shook his head emphatically. "Thank you for your kindness, but we will not go. If we go, who would tell the people here of Jesus? No, we will not be driven out by these evil men."

He waved an arm toward the blackened fields. "We will stay here and replant our crops. God is with us, and He will help us to rebuild our homes and our church again." Behind Eduardo, dark heads nodded solemn agreement.

It was getting late by the time the four Americans were ready to leave. Eduardo had agreed to let Alan fly the one badly injured woman to the health clinic in Magdalena. As they helped the injured woman and her mother and the baby into the helicopter, Justin saw Uncle Pete shove a roll of bills into Alan's hand.

Eduardo stared in disbelief when Alan returned an hour later with a load of blankets, sacks of flour, sugar, powdered milk—even a crate of live chickens.

As villagers crowded close to finger the bundles in amazed silence, Eduardo gave each of the Americans a hard *abrazo,* the traditional Bolivian hug. "I thank you on behalf of our people. We will never forget you."

As Alan translated, Eduardo added, "Please do not forget us, either. These men are evil and strong. It would be easy to give in and grow the coca. As you have seen, some Christians have already gone back to the coca fields. Pray that we may stay strong to follow Jesus."

Uncle Pete lifted their backpacks into the helicopter. "Hop in, kids! We'd better leave if we plan to make it home before dark."

"Hasta luego!" the twins called good-bye in halting Spanish.

Turning to go, a flicker of movement at the side of the road caught Justin's attention.

It was the man with the black leather jacket. He stood hidden in the long shadow the setting sun cast across the helicopter, his unfocused eyes closely watching the little group.

Justin grabbed Alan's arm and pointed. "There he is!" he said urgently. "That man's been following us. Ask Eduardo if he knows who he is."

Realizing he had been seen, the man dove into the tall brush that lined the other side of the road, but Alan had already pointed him out to Eduardo. The young man shook his head violently. Alan translated his agitated words.

"No, we do not know him. But can you not tell from his eyes what he is? That man is a *drogadicto*—one of the takers of the cocaine!"

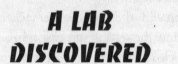

Chapter Seven

A LAB DISCOVERED

As THE camp helicopter lifted off, Jenny looked questioningly at Alan. "Why would those men burn everything down like that? It's just awful!"

Alan's mouth tightened. "It's not a new story. This is one reason it's so hard to stop cocaine production. If a farmer turns from coca to other crops, the cocaine dealers figure he has turned to be a police informer. Besides, they don't like any interference in their supply of coca leaf."

He waved toward the black and smoldering ruins below. "So they decided to teach your friends a lesson—and discourage anyone else from following their example."

"Well, I'm glad they decided to stay and stand up to those bullies!" Jenny answered forcefully.

"What I'd like to know is why that cocaine addict was following us," Justin said from his seat behind the pilot. "I wonder what he wanted?"

"He was probably a thief," Alan answered after Justin quickly filled him in on their past run-ins with the stranger in the black leather jacket. "Addicts often turn to stealing in order to buy drugs. Tourists are usually the easiest targets. At any rate, he can't possibly know where you've come from. I'm sure you've seen the last of him."

"I wonder," Justin muttered. Jenny looked back at him curiously, but he said nothing more.

It was dark by the time they reached the oil camp, but the helicopter lights and a faint glow from the lab building enabled Alan to set down on the field behind the camp buildings. The four quickly scrubbed off soot from the fire in the camp's makeshift shower and tumbled into bed. Justin remembered to pray for Mike and his search as he drifted off to sleep.

Justin was biting into a fresh, hot cinnamon roll the next morning when Dr. Latour and Rodrigo joined the group on the veranda. Justin secretly studied them as they pulled out chairs and sat down. The two men ate quickly without joining in the conversation and were finished eating while the others were still leisurely drinking a second pot of coffee. Dr. Latour rose abruptly, but before Rodrigo could follow, Jenny leaned over and asked, "Are you going to be working around here today?"

White teeth flashed as the young, dark assistant answered, *"Sí,* we will be in the lab all day. We have a lot of samples to process."

"Can we watch?" Jenny begged. "There's nothing else to do!"

"No, you may not!" Dr. Latour snapped before his assistant could answer. "Now, if you will excuse us . . ." He marched down the veranda steps. Rodrigo reluctantly put down his coffee cup and followed.

Uncle Pete drained his cup and stood up. "If you two are looking for something to do, you can help Alan sort through the office files."

"That's not exactly what I had in mind!" Jenny whispered to Justin, but the two children obediently followed Alan and Uncle Pete to the cinderblock office building across the gravel driveway.

Alan pulled out a key ring, but as he reached for the doorknob, he exclaimed, "That's strange! I know I left this door locked!"

He bent to examine the lock. Peering over his shoulder, Justin noticed that the wooden door stood slightly ajar. "It looks like it's been forced!"

Alan pushed the door open, then stood in dismay. Crowding up from behind, the twins saw that it looked like a small cyclone had gone through the office! The desk and file cabinet were tipped over, and the drawers were scattered across the floor. Pens, pencils, bottles, and other office items were scattered everywhere. A dried-up puddle of ink stained the tiles.

Alan stepped carefully over the shards of a glass container and looked around. Uncle Pete stepped up behind him. "Can you tell what's missing?"

"The files!" Alan answered immediately. "The ones with the test results and Dr. Latour's surveys. They're all gone!"

Justin suddenly realized what had been missing in the mess on the floor—there was no paper.

Dr. Latour was suddenly in the office door, Rodrigo behind him. "What is all the commotion?"

Taking in the situation with one glance, he said coolly, "It would appear that someone broke in here while you were gone yesterday."

"Everything was fine when I went to pick up the Parkers," Alan insisted. "Gerard, did you see any strangers around after I left?"

"No, I didn't." Dr. Latour answered firmly. "But Rodrigo and I didn't leave the lab until well after dark. Have you checked the other buildings for signs of a break-in?"

The twins trailed behind the adults as they checked through the camp. Their own bungalow was untouched, but Alan discovered scratch marks on his own lock that he hadn't noticed in the dark. Checking through his belongings, he found that a small radio and a pair of cufflinks were missing.

"It must have been a petty thief looking for cash," he decided at last. "But why would he take the files?"

"He obviously thought they might contain something worth selling," Dr. Latour answered curtly. "Now if you will excuse us, Rodrigo and I had better get started redoing those reports. This means a lot of extra work for us."

Uncle Pete raised his reddish-brown eyebrows. "But surely you keep copies of your reports. I had planned on checking out those survey sites today."

"I only keep rough notes in the lab. They wouldn't make any sense to you," Dr. Latour answered. "It would do no good to fly out there without the information in those reports. And it will take days to redo all the field work."

Surprisingly cheerful, considering he had lost several weeks of hard work, he added, "There is really no need for you to fly out to the survey sites personally. I know you had only planned on spending a few days here. Why don't you return home? I'll forward the surveys and test results as soon as I redo them. Then you can make your decision as to the future of this camp."

Uncle Pete nodded. "I'll think about it. In the meantime, Alan and I will get the office cleaned up."

"Fine," Dr. Latour answered crisply. "In that case, Rodrigo and I will return to work."

As Rodrigo and Dr. Latour turned to leave, Justin called out, "By the way, Dr. Latour, did you hear about the strange man that followed us on our trip? He turned out to be a cocaine addict."

Dr. Latour's broad back stiffened instantly. Justin saw him throw a startled glance at Rodrigo. He turned around slowly.

"No, I hadn't heard. You were fortunate that you suffered no harm." The two men stalked off in the direction of the lab.

"What was that all about?" Jenny asked.

"Just an idea I had," Justin whispered back.

The twins spent the next hour helping clean up the mess in the office. When they were done, Justin turned to Jenny, "Come on! I want to talk to Special Agent Turner."

They found the DEA agent outside the aluminum office building, loudly lecturing a guard who stood stiffly at attention, a gloomy look on his face. When he saw the twins, he dismissed the guard.

"Taking a *siesta* on duty! What kind of soldiers are they making these days?" Turning to Justin and Jenny, he demanded gruffly, "Okay, what is it this time?"

Justin told him about the break-in, and about the man who had followed them the day before. "Maybe you could arrest the guy and find out something that would help," he finished hopefully.

The DEA agent's stern expression lightened. "Thanks for

thinking of us, Justin. Any information is helpful at the moment. But I'm afraid we have no authority to arrest a man just because he is an addict. What we need is the man who is supplying the drug."

Justin's face fell, but Jenny suddenly added, "Maybe we *do* know something that will help!"

Justin brightened. "Yeah, Eduardo's village!" Special Agent Turner's gray eyes sharpened with interest as the twins filled him in on what had happened.

"It's unlikely we'd catch the guys now, but we'll pass the information on to the DEA office in Santa Cruz," he told them. "In the meantime, keep your eyes open. If you see that man again, or anything else of interest, let me know."

"We will!" Justin promised eagerly. At that moment, Mike emerged from one of the sleeping tents wearing his flying outfit. His black eyes lit up momentarily, but he scowled fiercely, "So, you're back again!"

He strode toward the helicopter. "I suppose you want another ride," he growled as he swung open the door. At Jenny's excited squeal, he continued sourly, "I thought so! Okay, get in. I don't have all day!"

Reaching down, he pulled Jenny up the steps. Justin hung back. "If you don't want us . . ." he said in what he hoped was a dignified tone.

"Who said I didn't want you?" Mike snapped. "I can use some extra pairs of eyes today. Get in!" In spite of his scowl, Justin decided that Mike really was glad to see them.

"Well, kids, we are as close to nailing that cocaine ring as the last time you were here," he said sarcastically as the rotor blades disturbed the still heat. "Do you still think God is going to help us catch them?"

"Yes, we do," Jenny answered firmly. "We've been praying for you, haven't we, Justin?"

"Well, you just keep on," Mike answered more softly. "I don't suppose it hurts anything. Anyway, I thought we'd track down that clearing we photographed on the last flight. That's why I need you. You kids keep your eyes peeled and let me know if you see a break in the trees. We're especially looking for anything long enough to be an airstrip."

An hour later, they had examined three natural clearings and a sugar cane farm. "Everything looks the same from up here!" Justin complained.

Slumped back in his seat, Mike was scowling again. "I told you praying wouldn't help. We're heading back to base!"

"Oh, couldn't we try just a little longer?" Jenny pleaded. "Look! There's another little clearing over there. It might be something important!"

"Someone else's farm," Mike muttered. "Okay, we'll give it fifteen minutes more."

A strong wind buffeted the helicopter and bent the tops of the trees as they swung over to the opening Jenny had spotted. As they hovered above the break in the trees, Justin saw that it was not really a clearing, but only an opening where the trees grew less densely. Raw stumps showed that some of the trees had recently been removed.

He swallowed hard with disappointment. As though reading his mind, Jenny said mournfully, "It's not a coca field *or* an airstrip. I guess we'd better give up."

"Just a minute!" Mike bent forward, staring intently into the thick foliage beyond the small clearing. His scowl suddenly disappeared, and there was a note of excitement in his voice. "I don't believe it! Kids, I think we may have hit the jackpot!"

They swung leisurely away from the opening in the trees. A strong gust of wind again tossed the trees below, and Justin saw what Mike had seen—a glimpse of what could be olive-green canvas. It would normally be invisible under the thick leaf cover.

He gulped. "You mean there might be a cocaine lab down there?"

Mike nodded. He turned the helicopter away from the site. "Those were camouflage tents down there. Not the sort of thing the average family around here owns."

Jenny spoke up. "But we didn't find an airstrip. How can there be a lab?"

Mike pointed out the window. "That must be the answer. There's a four-wheel-drive track hidden under those trees."

Below, Justin could trace a faint line through the jungle that might possibly be a road. As Mike flew on, the territory they covered began to look vaguely familiar. "That track goes to the coca farm!" he exclaimed.

Mike nodded approvingly. "That's right. And there's a passable dirt road from there out to the main road. But they still have to fly their goods out of the area. I wonder how? We've got every known airstrip covered."

"Are we going to land?" Jenny asked eagerly.

"No!" Mike was now the professional DEA agent. "If that is a cocaine lab down there, the workers will be armed and dangerous. I want you kids to stay out of this."

Seeing their downcast expression, he added, "You don't think *I'm* stupid enough to go down alone either do you? I'm radioing for help."

He was already on the radios. When he set the microphone down, he turned to his passengers. "Special Agent Turner will be sending UMOPAR troops right away. I've given them coordinates for finding that road. I'm heading back to base now to pick up the DEA agent and some men."

"Won't they get away by the time you get there?" Justin asked anxiously.

"Why do you think I flew on by?" Mike explained reasonably. "That place is practically invisible from the air. We've flown over the area half-a-dozen times and never seen a thing. They have no reason to think we've seen anything this time.

"And we wouldn't have, if the wind hadn't been blowing right when we were over the spot." The young agent was actually smiling. "Maybe there *is* something to that praying business."

A half hour later, they approached the oil company property. Below them, billows of dust masked the rutted dirt road that led past the two camps. Mike dropped low, and the dust cloud separated into a pair of army jeeps and the transport truck Justin had seen parked beside the DEA office. Soldiers in khaki uniforms, machine guns and rifles slung over their backs, waved as the helicopter swooped down over their heads.

"They're on the way!" Mike announced jubilantly. "Those filthy drug dealers won't get away this time. Come on, let's pick up the boss!"

The DEA agent, four armed UMOPAR agents at his back, was waiting impatiently beside the helicopter landing. As Mike set the helicopter down, he ran toward them, one arm sheltering his face from the strong wind of the rotors. He was aboard almost before the helicopter touched the ground. The other men scrambled through the open door at his heels.

Afraid he would be ordered out, Justin made himself as small as possible. He noticed that Jenny was also holding her breath, but the DEA agent didn't even glance at the twins as Mike lifted off within seconds of landing. The soldiers squatted on the floor while the DEA agent gave orders in Spanish. One man was hooking a coil of nylon rope to a thick metal rod above the door.

"What's that for?" Jenny whispered in her brother's ear. But she soon found out as Mike headed back to the tiny clearing. The wind had died down, and there was no sign of human habitation below. But Mike easily maneuvered the helicopter to a position near the glimpse of camouflage they had seen earlier.

Lowering the helicopter, he hovered barely above tree level while one of the soldiers slid open the door and tossed out the coils of rope. Seated closest to the door, Justin was glad he wore a seatbelt as he glimpsed the ground far below the widespread branches.

The soldier who had tossed out the rope snapped a hook on his belt to the rope and slid over the edge. One by one, the others followed, skillfully dodging branches, their weapons carefully balanced across their backs. When the last one hit the ground, Special Agent Turner slammed the door.

"They'll guard the place until the main troops arrive," he informed Mike. Then he seemed to notice the children for the first time.

"What are you doing here?" he bellowed. "You should have been dropped off at the base. This isn't a school picnic we're on!"

He looked so stern that Justin was sure he would order Mike to take them home. But after a long moment, he shrugged. "Well, we don't have time to take you back now. You'll have to come along."

Justin and Jenny couldn't suppress excited grins. As he buckled himself into the copilot's seat, Special Agent Turner warned gruffly, "Don't get any funny ideas about seeing action. You'll stay in the chopper with Mike, well out of the way of any trouble."

But as they circled back across the small opening in the trees, Mike exclaimed angrily, "Sir, didn't you tell those clowns to stay out of sight and keep quiet?"

"I sure did," the DEA agent answered grimly.

He leaned forward as Mike moved in for a closer look. An area just large enough to land a helicopter had been completely logged off. Two men stood in the center, their uniforms clearly marking them as members of the UMOPAR team they had dropped off fifteen minutes earlier. They waved violently as the helicopter hovered overhead, and a flow of Spanish blasted from the radio.

Special Agent Turner nodded grimly to Mike. "There's a cocaine lab down there all right, but the place was abandoned by the time our men got here."

"What? That's impossible!" Mike burst out.

Striking the armrest of his seat with a blow of his clenched fist, he swore so loudly and viciously that Justin had to strain to hear as the DEA agent added, "Both the men and the cocaine are gone. I'm sorry Mike!"

Chapter Eight

NIGHTMARE CREATURE

"Set her down, Mike!" Special Agent Turner commanded. "We're going in!"

Mike carefully maneuvered into the tiny opening below. Special Agent Turner had the door open and was following the two UMOPAR men into the underbrush before Justin managed to unbuckle his seatbelt. Jerking off his earphones, Mike barked, "You kids stay with me and keep out of trouble!"

Justin looked around. A dozen yards beyond the clearing, a bunk tent of dappled olive-green and brown canvas hid under a thick grove of trees. Green walls of heavy screen stood about four feet high, while the peaked roof allowed room for a man to stand upright. Through the open tent flap, Justin could see a line of camp cots inside.

Mike was examining the small patch of cleared ground around the helicopter. "We aren't the first helicopter to land here!" he said with satisfaction. "No wonder we haven't found signs of an airstrip. They've been taking the cocaine out by helicopter!"

"This could be a real clue. There aren't many helicopters in Bolivia. If we could trace their recent whereabouts . . ."

A clear picture of the oil camp helicopter suddenly popped into Justin's mind. It would fit easily into this space. Mike straightened up. "Okay, let's go! You two stay right behind me and keep your hands in your pockets."

Carefully picking his way across fallen branches, Justin followed Jenny and Mike around the bunk tent and soon noticed two buildings made of wood planks—one the size of their tool shed back home, the other several times bigger. Camouflage nets kept them from being seen from more than a few yards away.

Mike strode over to a picnic table that sat under overhanging branches in between the buildings. He seemed to have forgotten the twins, but they trailed obediently behind.

The table had been set for a dozen men, and a half-eaten meal sat on the plates. A coffee mug lay on its side, its contents forming a dark-brown pool on the weathered wood. Mike picked up a tall metal glass and looked inside.

"There's still ice in here!" he shouted in disgust. "They must have left in the last half hour."

"Mike! We found the lab!" Special Agent Turner exclaimed, thrusting his head out the doorway of the larger building. Dropping the glass, Mike joined him, the twins close behind. Peering into the gloomy building, they saw a long, dark room full of unfamiliar objects.

The jeeps and transport truck bounced into the clearing minutes later, and soon the area was swarming with armed men. The DEA agent had discovered a portable electric generator and lights now brightened the largest building.

Jenny had slipped out to explore the rest of the camp, but Justin was more interested in the strange equipment that several

UMOPAR agents were now taking apart. The DEA agent stood over a metal frame the shape and size of a dining table.

Suspended from the frame was a thick white cloth, like a bed sheet, giving it the look of a sunken trampoline.

"What's this for?" Justin asked. In answer, Special Agent Turner rubbed his fingers against the cloth, then held out his hand. Justin looked closely at the white powder that clung to it.

"This is the filter for the cocaine," the DEA agent explained. "Those leaves you saw the other day are turned into a paste we call cocaine base. The base is brought here and filtered with chemicals through this cloth until it turns into white crystals."

He motioned across the room to where a dozen heat lamps hung over a long wooden table. "The crystals are spread out under those to dry, then packaged."

His expression grew hard. "The final step in the process is smuggling it out to the U.S. and other countries to ruin the lives of millions of people!"

He was interrupted as Jenny bounced in the door. "There isn't anything very interesting out there," she announced. "That other building is just the kitchen. But you wouldn't believe what they found hidden in the bushes—a great big freezer and even a clothes dryer!"

She looked around the big room with interest. "What's all this?"

She bent over the filter, then glanced at the DEA agent. "Oh, I forgot! They found a whole bunch of garbage cans hidden behind the kitchen, too—way back in the brush. You know, those big plastic ones of all different colors."

She wrinkled her nose in disgust. "They smelled awful! The

soldiers were acting all excited, but they wouldn't let me take even one little peek inside!"

Justin grinned. If he knew his sister, she was probably going crazy with curiosity. Mike straightened up from a jumble of bottles and boxes he was sorting. "Did you say garbage cans?" he asked. "I wonder . . ."

But two soldiers were already carrying in two large orange pails. They set them on the floor, and Mike tore off the plastic lids.

"Chemicals for producing cocaine!" he announced. "And illegal to own in Bolivia. There must be thousands of dollars worth here!"

A bleak expression wiped the triumph from his face. "But there's no sign of the cocaine nor any evidence that points to those in charge. If we had caught just one of the workers!"

He slammed a fist into the palm of his other hand. "How could they have cleared out of here so fast? We *had* them! I know I didn't give anything away when I flew over."

Jenny piped up, "Maybe they overheard the radio."

Such scorn blazed from Mike's black eyes that Jenny stepped back. "Not unless they had the equipment to bypass half-a-dozen scrambling devices. No, they were warned! But how?"

He was interrupted by a soldier in lieutenant's uniform who mumbled something in his ear. Mike turned to the DEA agent, "Sir, we've detained the coca grower. He insists he doesn't know anything about the lab—or the track that leads here. He says he just sold his crop to strangers who offered him a good price. Do you want us to hold him?"

Special Agent Turner nodded his head. "I have a feeling he knows more than he's telling. I'll interview him myself."

He marched toward the door. "We've gone over everything there is to see here. We'll leave the UMOPAR agents—they will go through the area with a fine-tooth comb. Pick out a dozen good men to stand guard just in case someone comes back. And get those kids back to the oil camp before someone starts worrying."

Deep, bitter lines again grooved Mike's face as he hurried the twins into the helicopter. He was so obviously lost in his own angry thoughts that neither twin dared say a word on the flight back to camp. Dropping them off in the field behind the camp buildings, he took off again without a glance in their direction.

There was no one in sight as they came around the back of the administration building, but the camp jeep stood at the door of the lab. As they sauntered down the gravel driveway that divided the property, Rodrigo walked down the lab steps.

"Hi, there!" Jenny called gaily.

Visibly startled, Rodrigo stumbled on the bottom step, dropping a bundle of what looked like burlap bags. "Wh—what are you doing here?" he gasped.

Recovering himself, he picked up his bundle and tossed it into the back of the jeep. "I thought you kids were gone for the day," he added more calmly.

Jenny looked around. "Where's Uncle Pete and Alan?"

Rodrigo glanced nervously behind him. "They left right after you did—took the camp helicopter."

He reached into his pocket and pulled out a folded piece of notebook paper. "Here, they left you a message."

Justin leaned over the back of the jeep. Besides Rodrigo's bundle of sacks, there was only a folded canvas tarp, of the type used to protect cargo from the weather, and a large metal tool chest.

"Did you hear about the raid on the cocaine lab?" Justin asked, watching the lab assistant closely. "Things got so hot we had to come home."

"Yes . . . yes, we did." Rodrigo didn't look at all well. He glanced toward the lab again.

Dr. Latour loomed up behind Rodrigo. "What nonsense are you kids talking about?"

"The DEA just raided a cocaine lab," Justin answered.

"We were there and saw it all. They didn't catch anyone, though. Someone warned them before the DEA got there."

"Rodrigo said you already knew," Jenny added brightly. "How did you find out? I didn't think anyone else was back."

Casting an annoyed glance at Rodrigo, Dr. Latour said sharply, "We haven't heard anything. But when the entire complement of UMOPAR goes out the front gate armed to the teeth, there's obviously more than a drill going on!"

Without another word, the chief geologist pushed past the children and climbed into the driver's seat of the camp jeep. Avoiding eye contact with the children, Rodrigo climbed over the tailgate and began shuffling through the tool chest. Peering over the side, Justin opened his eyes wide as he glimpsed what looked like a semiautomatic rifle. Dr. Latour snapped a curt order, and Rodrigo slammed the lid shut.

"Where are you going?" Jenny asked as Rodrigo sat down. "It might be dangerous out there with all those cocaine dealers on the loose."

Dr. Latour was so angry that his hands shook as he turned

the ignition key. "You are far too nosy, kid!" he hissed. "Mind your own business or you'll find yourself in a lot of trouble!"

"What got into him?" Jenny asked, staring after the speeding jeep. "He didn't even ask about the drug raid. You'd think he'd want to know!"

Justin watched as Rodrigo climbed out to unlock the gate, then he grinned at his sister. "Not everyone is as nosy as you!"

"You're the one who's always poking your nose into things!" Jenny gave her brother a playful push that sent him sprawling into the gravel driveway.

"Okay, you asked for it!" Picking up a handful of pebbles, Justin jumped to his feet and chased after his sister. Jenny was a fast runner, but she was laughing so hard that he soon caught up. As he dumped the handful of gravel down the neck of her T-shirt, he pushed Dr. Latour and Rodrigo's strange behavior to the back of his mind.

The note Rodrigo had given them told Justin and Jenny to stay put if they got back before Uncle Pete and Alan and that the two men planned to be back for supper. The twins ate lunch alone, then leafed through magazines on their bungalow veranda, keeping an eye out for either the helicopter or the jeep.

The sun was setting as Uncle Pete and Alan finally flew in. The twins were now accustomed to eating supper at eight o'clock or later. Jenny was still recounting her version of the morning's adventures between mouthfuls of a sticky custard dessert, when Justin heard the familiar roar of the jeep engine. He kept one eye on the front of the lab as he ate, but the headlights of the camp jeep never appeared in the driveway. *They must have circled around back,* he decided.

"You kids stay away from the DEA camp until we leave," Uncle Pete ordered when Jenny had finished. "They'll be up to their ears in work over there."

Jenny nodded, then asked, "When *are* we leaving?"

Justin looked up from his dessert in dismay. "We aren't leaving yet, are we, Uncle Pete?"

Uncle Pete raised his eyebrows. "I hadn't planned on it. I haven't finished my investigation."

"But I thought you couldn't!" Jenny said. "I mean, with all those reports and things stolen . . ."

Uncle Pete's green eyes twinkled. "Don't you worry about that! I have all the information I need."

He didn't add anything more, and Justin and Jenny soon excused themselves and returned to the bungalow. They had exhausted Alan's pile of old magazines, so Justin pulled out a set of checkers. But after two games, both of them decided to call it a night. Uncle Pete and Alan were still bent over a sheet of scribbled numbers when the twins called a goodnight from the office door.

Back in the bungalow, Justin spread toothpaste on his toothbrush and poured a glass from the pitcher of boiled water the cook had provided. With the tropical heat, he and Jenny had traded the sweat suits they used as pajamas for shorts and T-shirts.

"You can have first dibs on the outhouse, Jenny," he called as he brushed his teeth. "The flashlight's right here."

Jenny emerged from her bedroom. Accepting the flashlight he offered, she opened the front door and hesitated. "It's awfully dark out there. Why don't you come with me, Justin?"

Surprised, Justin demanded, "Why? You've always gone by yourself before!"

Jenny lifted her shoulders. "I know, but . . . today's been kind of spooky and all . . . and anyone could be out there. Maybe that man's still following . . . or one of those cocaine dealers. Please come!"

"Don't be such a sissy!" Justin scolded, but he reluctantly followed her out to the veranda.

"Girls!" he muttered under his breath as he took the flashlight Jenny shoved at him. Walking single file behind his sister, he made a narrow path of light for their feet.

The outhouse sat in a patch of beaten-down brush about a hundred yards behind their bungalow. Justin had gotten used to the long trip, but even he had to admit he preferred the walk by day. A three-quarter moon lit the open spaces with silver, but the bushes and trees loomed black and menacing. It reminded him of younger years when he and Jenny had played in their own back yard after dark, imagining monsters or enemies behind every bush. But then, safety had been only as far away as the warm, shining light of their kitchen door.

The night seemed unusually loud, with strange rustles and noises. Justin couldn't suppress a shiver as something dropped at his feet. Jenny slipped a hand into his as he turned the flashlight downward. An oversized toad blinked up at him. With a deep croak, it was gone.

He was relieved when the familiar form of the outhouse was before them. Twice the size of a telephone booth, it was built of locally cut planks of wood, somewhat carelessly nailed together. Although fairly new, tropical storms and sun had already weathered the boards to a silvery gray. A rusty latch held shut a rickety handmade door.

"See, I told you there was nothing to be scared of!" Justin told his sister. "Go on in. I'll wait right here."

Jenny opened the outhouse door. The interior was inky black. Justin handed her the flashlight She stepped inside and closed the door, and Justin leaned against the weathered doorjamb to wait. Then a terrified scream shattered the night!

Justin yanked open the door as Jenny stumbled backward. "Don't tell me you've seen another scorpion," he sighed loudly, catching her as she half-fell down the one high step. His eyes followed the narrow beam of the flashlight, and suddenly his own heart skipped a beat.

Against the back wall of the outhouse was a square wooden box the size of a toilet. A hole in the top led to the pit below, and on top of this had been fastened a regular plastic seat taken off of a discarded toilet.

The toilet lid leaned up against the wall. Over the top, curling and uncurling like grasping claws, reached two pair of black, hairy legs. As the twins watched in frozen fascination, the toilet lid crashed down with a force that wrung another scream from Jenny and a startled yelp from Justin.

For there—with eyes glittering gold in the flashlight beam, its circular, mouse-sized body humped high, and its eight hairy legs extending the width of the toilet lid—squatted a creature straight out of a nightmare!

Chapter Nine

EVIDENCE DISCOVERED!

JUSTIN AND Jenny stood frozen for a long moment as the creature reared, its velvety front legs clawing the air. A beak-like mouth snapped, and they caught sight of fangs like those of a rattlesnake. Justin pulled Jenny away from the door. "Stay out of there," he ordered hoarsely, "I'll get a stick."

But someone else had heard Jenny's scream. Uncle Pete was already pushing past them, and they heard the sound of heavy blows. Then Uncle Pete appeared in the doorway of the outhouse, and Jenny threw herself into his arms. Alan appeared moments later, demanding breathlessly, "What happened? Has anyone been hurt?"

Alan shone his flashlight around the interior of the outhouse. "It's okay, kids!" he assured them. "It's only a tarantula spider. They look awful, but they aren't really that poisonous. One that size would certainly give you a bite you'd remember, but they aren't deadly."

Peering around Uncle Pete's arm, Jenny looked unconvinced. With the branch Uncle Pete had used to kill it, Alan swept the tarantula out onto the path. The giant spider now lay on its back, its furry legs curled unmoving over its body.

Justin bent down to study the ugly creature. It looked much smaller now than he had remembered.

Alan, too, bent over the spider. He looked puzzled. "I don't understand how this happened, kids. We always keep that door latched, and I was just out here myself an hour ago."

Nudging the creature with the toe of his shoe, he shook his head in amazement. "I've heard of tarantulas this big in the deep jungle, but I've never seen one around here!"

"Well, I hate spiders, and I'm not staying here if there are anymore of those around!" Jenny cried. She was still clinging to Uncle Pete.

"What exactly is going on here?" a smooth voice demanded. Startled, Justin jumped to his feet as the tall form of Dr. Latour loomed out of the dark. Justin stifled a momentary suspicion as he caught the look of genuine surprise on the geologist's face. The look turned to cool amusement as he took in the spider and Jenny's face, still wet with tears.

"Mr. Parker, it's evident that your family isn't cut out for the jungle," he said. "I suggest you all go home before you run into something much worse than a spider. I'd be glad to run you in to Trinidad."

Uncle Pete's voice was suddenly cold as ice. "Are you suggesting that I drop my investigation, Dr. Latour?"

Dr. Latour's cool gray eyes narrowed as he answered. "As I've said before, there is nothing more you can do at the moment. I've already told you what the situation is here. You've found nothing in the records that shows my analysis to be at fault."

"I would have to agree," Uncle Pete answered dryly, "since most of the records are unfortunately unavailable!"

Looking deeply offended, Dr. Latour demanded, "Are you suggesting I had something to do with that?" He drew himself up arrogantly. "You know my reputation! Have you any possible reason to doubt my commitment to finding oil for Triton and for this needy country?"

"No, I don't," Uncle Pete admitted. He dropped his gaze to his nephew and niece.

"Well, Justin, Jenny, what do you think? Are you ready to pack it in and go home?"

"No!" Justin's answer exploded in the silence. He continued more quietly, "Please, Uncle Pete! I want to stay."

"Well, I'd just as soon go . . ." Jenny said with quivering voice. She stopped as Justin caught her eye; he was shaking his head violently. "I . . . I mean I guess I'd like to stay, too."

Uncle Pete nodded. "That settles it. We'll finish this investigation from here."

Dr. Latour seemed annoyed, but he shrugged his broad shoulders. "It's your decision."

🦎

The lights were out across camp when Justin slipped into Jenny's small bedroom. The faint moonlight entering through the open shutter showed Jenny still sitting cross-legged on her camp cot.

When she saw her brother, she demanded, "What's the big idea? Why did you make me say we'd stay? It's not like there's anything to do here!"

Justin sat down on the edge of the cot. "Because," he said

calmly, "I think something funny is going on here—and I know Uncle Pete thinks so too. I don't want to go until we find out what it is."

With the practice of years, Jenny instantly read his mind. "You mean Dr. Latour, don't you?"

Justin nodded. "Dr. Latour seems awfully anxious to get us out of here. And I think I know why. I'm pretty sure he and Rodrigo are mixed up in the drug traffic."

Jenny dropped her brush in astonishment. "What makes you think *that?*" She added suspiciously, "I hope you aren't going to start in again about seeing Dr. Latour in those pictures!"

Justin looked stubborn. "Well, what if it *was* him? Don't you think it's strange that there's a track leading from the cocaine lab right to that field? Besides, he was so angry about the DEA being here."

Thinking of the look he had seen on the geologist's face, he added, "I got the impression that . . . well, that he almost hated them! Then other things started adding up."

Justin ticked the points off on his fingers. "First, do you remember what we overheard that night? He didn't want us snooping around because he had 'one last haul' to make.

"Then there's that man who's been following us. All right, maybe he was just a thief, but he never did try to steal anything from us! And we heard Rodrigo say he was going to have someone keep an eye on us. Who better than a drug addict, if they really are mixed up in cocaine dealing?"

Jenny still wasn't convinced. "If this is all true, why hasn't the DEA found out about it? They saw those pictures too!"

"Mr. Turner said they'd never actually met Dr. Latour or

Rodrigo. Those two have been very careful to stay away from the DEA camp," Justin answered. "And don't forget Dr. Latour's perfect record. There's no reason to suspect him."

Leaning back against the wall, Justin continued, "This morning, Mike said the cocaine was going out by helicopter. Alan told me the other day that the oil camp had the only helicopter in this area. I got to thinking about how easy it would be for Dr. Latour to fly in there and get cocaine out."

"So that's why you asked Rodrigo about the raid!" Jenny exclaimed. "If they saw all the soldiers going by, I suppose Dr. Latour could have called the lab and warned them there might be a raid."

"That's right!" Justin said. "Remember my friend Nick back home? His dad is a big businessman who travels places like the Middle East and some of those way-out African countries, and he has a sat-phone just like that one in the lab. He showed it to us. It can reach anywhere—much less some jungle lab! Maybe the lab had a sat-phone, too. And then, the way they took off this afternoon . . . Where did they go? And what were all those burlap bags for? Maybe they were meeting someone."

He made his last point. "And finally, how *did* that tarantula get in the outhouse? I was in there myself after supper, and I shut the door. Dr. Latour and Rodrigo are always exploring out in the jungle. . . ."

"Then you think Dr. Latour put that spider in the outhouse?" Jenny asked doubtfully.

Justin shook his head. "That isn't his style. Besides, he looked awfully surprised. No, I think that was Rodrigo's idea. Remember when he told Dr. Latour he could get rid of us? He must think we're real sissies!"

"Well, a spider that big would scare anyone!" Jenny declared, shame-faced. She added, "But I can't imagine Rodrigo being mixed up in something like that. He seems so nice!"

"You just think that because he kisses your hand and all that stuff!" Justin answered scornfully.

"Well, it still seems to me you're doing a lot of guessing," Jenny replied. "And if you're right, what can you do about it? We got into enough trouble poking into things *last* time."

"Yeah, I know!" Justin admitted. "I'm going to tell Uncle Pete about this. If he thinks there's something to it, he'll check it out and tell Special Agent Turner."

He opened the door. Hearing a steady snore, he added with a grin, "I'll tell him in the morning, that is!"

A tap on the shoulder awoke Justin the next morning. Opening bleary eyes, he saw that it was still dark. Uncle Pete bent over his cot and whispered, "Justin, Alan and I are leaving to check out the rest of those survey sites. This should finish the investigation. You and Jenny stay out of trouble while we're gone."

"Sure, Uncle Pete," Justin answered sleepily, burrowing back into his pillow. Then he was suddenly wide awake.

"Oh, Uncle Pete, I wanted to tell you . . ." It was too late. The screen door banged shut behind his uncle, and moments later he heard the camp helicopter lift overhead.

The first weak rays of dawn provided enough light for Justin to find his clothes. Shaking them out, he dressed quickly, then woke his sister.

"What do we do now?" she asked with dismay. Justin shrugged. "We can at least look around a little—just to see if Dr. Latour and Rodrigo brought anything back last night."

"Not until after breakfast," Jenny said firmly. Justin nodded agreement, but as the twins stepped onto the veranda, Justin heard the sound of an engine.

"Get down!" he hissed, pulling Jenny down behind the veranda railing as Rodrigo backed the camp jeep around to the front steps of the lab.

"Why?" Jenny hissed back.

"I want to see what they're up to!" As Rodrigo disappeared inside, Justin swung a leg over the railing. "You wait here. I'll be right back!"

Out of sight of anyone who might be looking out the lab windows, he moved quietly to the back of the jeep. He was back within a minute. "Nothing in there," he announced triumphantly. "Not even those bags they loaded yesterday. If they did bring anything back last night, it's still inside."

The twins ducked down again as the lab door opened. Though unable to see, the two children could hear footsteps on the gravel and Dr. Latour's voice raised in anger.

"How dare they take off without notifying us! We've got to have that chopper!"

"Why not just wait until they return?" replied Rodrigo in accented English.

"With the DEA swarming all over? No, we've got to get that stuff out this morning."

Rodrigo muttered something, and Dr. Latour's voice rose again. "Yes, you were so sure you could get rid of them. When you said you had a plan, I thought you had something a little more subtle than that stupid spider. I had a collector willing to pay big money for that thing!"

Justin nudged his sister, then strained to hear as Rodrigo answered gloomily, "Well, at least they're gone for a few hours."

"No thanks to you! We'd better move things out before they get back."

"It would save a lot of time to make our calls from here."

"Are you kidding? This is one day when the DEA will be monitoring every radio broadcast and cell-phone transmission in the Beni!" Dr. Latour answered. "You do know they can triangulate the position of a broadcast or cell-phone transmission right down to a mile or two. No, I want us well off Triton property when we make those calls."

The engine started again, and the men's voices could no longer be heard. The twins waited until the jeep had faded from hearing before they came out from hiding.

"Boy, it *does* sound like they're up to something!" Jenny admitted. "Maybe we'd better go tell Mike and Mr. Turner about this."

"No, not yet!" Justin shook his head. "We still need proof. We can't call Mr. Turner over here just because we heard those guys talking."

He disappeared inside the bungalow. A few moments later he emerged, camera in hand. He handed his sister a spare roll of film. "Here, can you hold on to this?"

"What's it for?" Jenny asked as she tucked the film into a jeans pocket.

"I want to see what those guys are in such a hurry to get rid of. And I want to take some pictures. Remember how Mr. Turner said they can't touch the cocaine dealers unless they actually catch them in the act?"

"Sure. So what?"

Justin slung the camera around his neck. "So if they haul off whatever they've got hidden before we can get Mr. Turner, we've got to have some proof it was there!"

"And what if Dr. Latour and Rodrigo come back before you're done? They think we're gone for the day."

Justin shrugged. "So we're just a couple of kids out exploring!"

Jenny shook her head doubtfully. "I don't know. It sounds dangerous!"

Justin suddenly remembered Eduardo's burning village. "I don't care!" he declared. "Those cocaine dealers need to be stopped! If I can do something to help, I will!"

"Besides," he added more calmly. "I figure it'll take them at least an hour to go make that radio call. . . ."

Jenny was suddenly excited. "Wouldn't it be wonderful if we *did* find some kind of proof? Mike would see that God really does answer our prayers!"

Forgetting about breakfast, she added impatiently, "Well, where do we start?"

"The lab!" Justin answered. "Dr. Latour and Rodrigo are the only ones who ever go in there. Come on!"

Jenny at his heels, he trotted across the gravel and up the lab steps. Then he stopped in sudden dismay. Thrust through the latch of the sturdy wood door was an oversized, shiny new padlock. He glanced at the large window to the right of the door. Its heavy wooden shutters were pulled tight, the black metal bars protecting them from prying fingers.

Turning to Jenny, he hunched his shoulders in disappointment. "We can't even get a look inside!"

"Well, you didn't really think they'd be stupid enough to leave anything out where we could see it, did you?" Jenny answered.

Justin smiled wistfully. "No, but I was hoping."

"Besides," Jenny added triumphantly, "we didn't have any problem seeing in the other night."

"Of course!" Justin exclaimed. "That hole in the back window. Come on!"

He led the way around to the back. There was nothing beyond the lab except open field and the shimmering metal roof of the DEA office building in the distance. The brush grew tall and thick here against the back wall, except for the narrow path that feet had pounded out toward the DEA camp.

As they neared the back window, the twins saw that the tangled bushes they'd crouched under three nights before were trampled and broken, as though by heavy boots. A double line of crushed grass indicated a track where a vehicle might have pulled up to the window.

Justin examined the faint track. "This must be where they parked the jeep last night."

Jenny was already inspecting the back window. "Look at this!" she cried excitedly. "They've taken off the bars!"

Justin joined her at the window. From a distance, everything had looked normal. But now Justin could see that the black bars that had protected the window were only leaning up against the wooden shutters. Crumbling holes in the plaster around the window showed where they had been forcibly removed. As on the front window, the heavy shutters were closed tightly, but at the bottom left-hand corner was the hole where something had eaten away at the wood.

"Why would they go to all this trouble when all they had to do was open the front door?" Jenny asked curiously.

"So we wouldn't see them unloading, of course!" Justin stated proudly, lifting the bars down and stacking them against the whitewashed wall. "This means they really *did* bring something in last night that they didn't want anyone to see. They brought it back here and passed it through the window."

The bottom of the window was level with Justin's chin. He put an eye to the hole, but blackness filled the interior of the lab. "You can't see a thing through here," he informed his sister.

Standing on tiptoes, he pushed hard at the shutters, but they didn't budge. "Must be barred from the inside," he commented. "I'm going to climb up and see if I can get them open."

The shutters fit into a wooden window frame. At the bottom of the frame was a windowsill about six inches wide. With both arms on the sill, Justin tried to haul himself up. But as he applied his whole weight to the wood, he heard a crack. A section of wood gave way under his hands, and he tumbled backward into the bushes.

"Great!" Jenny exclaimed as he scrambled to his feet. "Now you've broken the window."

Justin picked up the piece of wood and turned it over. "No, I didn't break it," he said in an odd tone. "Look! It's been cut!"

Jenny took the piece of wood from his hand and examined it closely. About a foot long, its sides were smooth and showed marks of a saw. Justin reached up and felt along the window. "There's room under here to hide something.

"See? This wood fits right over, so no one can see it." He reached inside a small hollow. "Here it is!" He pulled out a rectangular, plastic-covered object and handed it to Jenny. Jenny quickly unwrapped it. Inside the plastic was a small, leather-bound notebook.

"Rodrigo was writing in a notebook just like this the night we came," Jenny commented, flipping through its pages. "Remember how he hid it away when Dr. Latour took us into the lab?"

Justin studied the notebook over her shoulder. Small, precise writing covered the pages with numbers, slashes, letters, and an occasional name. There were no words. He handed it to Jenny. "It's just jumbled-up letters and numbers!"

"Maybe it's in code," Jenny suggested.

"Well, it must be important or it wouldn't be hidden like that. We'll take it for evidence," Justin decided. He tucked the notebook into his belt and pulled his shirt down to hide it.

"I still want to see inside the lab, though. If they bothered taking those bars down last night, then they certainly weren't hauling some experiment. It must be something illegal . . . maybe the stuff that disappeared from the cocaine lab."

Justin climbed back onto the window ledge, but he couldn't budge the heavy shutters. "We'll just have to make this hole bigger," he said at last. "I've got my penknife, and this wood's half-rotten anyway. Jenny, why don't you go get the flashlight?"

By the time Jenny returned with the flashlight, Justin had whittled away enough of the termite-eaten wood for him to put his arm through. Finding a good-sized rock to stand on, he leaned carefully against the sill and thrust the flashlight through the hole. He gave a low whistle as he saw what lay in the beam of the flashlight.

"We were right!" he announced excitedly as he slid down. Handing Jenny the flashlight, he moved aside to let her step up on the stone. She, too, whistled when she saw what he had seen. A dozen burlap sacks filled to overflowing leaned up against the back wall. Right under the window, one stood open. Its contents had obviously been under inspection, because several plastic bags filled with a white, powdery substance lay scattered on the top.

"That looks just like that white stuff on the cocaine filter Mr. Turner showed us," Jenny exclaimed as she handed the flashlight back to Justin.

"It must be the cocaine from the lab we saw yesterday," Justin agreed. "This'll cheer up Mike!"

He flashed his light around the lab. "They must have warned their men in time to get it away. And when they left in such a hurry yesterday afternoon, they were on their way to pick it up. They can't know anyone suspects them, but they must be going crazy having all this stuff here—especially with visitors in the camp. No wonder they wanted us to leave!"

Jenny moved away from the window. "We'd better get out of here before they come back. Let's find Mr. Turner and let him take care of it."

"Just a minute," Justin answered as he removed his camera from around his neck. "We've got to get pictures."

It was now fully daylight, but he set the flash for the dark lab interior, then maneuvered the camera through the hole. Though he couldn't see what he was shooting, he slowly moved the camera in a half-circle, taking one shot after another until he was sure he had photographed the whole room. He finished off with at least half-a-dozen shots of the open burlap bag.

He had just heard the click that meant the roll was finished when Jenny said urgently, "They're coming back, Justin! I can hear the jeep. Hurry!"

Justin looked up in dismay. "Already?"

The camera stuck as he pulled his arm out, and he lost precious seconds before he managed to tug it free. Hurriedly, he rewound the film, yanked open the back of the camera, and pulled it out. Taking the fresh roll from his sister's pocket, he quickly fitted it into the camera.

He thrust the camera into Jenny's hands and whispered, "Quick! Take some pictures! *Any* pictures!" Turning back to the window, he swiftly put the cut section of sill back into place. Leaning the bars up again, he brushed the wood splinters from the sill.

"Let's go before they see us!" he ordered urgently, reaching for the camera as Jenny snapped a final shot. But it was too late. Rodrigo was already striding around the side of the building.

He came to a surprised halt when he saw the children. He wore his usual bland smile, but his dark eyes darted suspiciously from one to the other. "What are you kids doing here? I thought you were gone for the day!"

"We were just out taking a few pictures," Justin answered calmly as the twins edged backward. But they hadn't taken two steps before Rodrigo caught sight of the freshly widened hole in the shutter. The smile disappeared as he lunged for the children.

"Boss!" he shouted. "These kids have been snooping in the lab!"

Chapter Ten

THE PURSUIT

"COME ON!" Justin whispered. "We've got to get this stuff to Special Agent Turner."

Grabbing his sister's hand, he turned to run—and collided with a solid object. He looked up to see Dr. Latour, dark with anger, looming over him. Steel-strong hands bit into Justin's shoulders.

"What do you think you're doing here?" the geologist asked, giving Justin a hard shake.

"We . . . we were just taking pictures," Justin said, trying to appear calm.

Steely-gray eyes seemed to bore right through his thin clothes to the notebook and film he had hidden. Then Dr. Latour released Justin so suddenly that he almost fell. Stepping over to the broken shutter, he examined it with a frown. Justin was too shaken to move, and before he had a chance to recover, Dr. Latour was back at his side.

"I don't think they could see anything," he informed Rodrigo. "It's pitch dark in there."

His anger seemed to have evaporated, and he was smiling as he turned back to the children. "Do forgive us," he said. "My assistant has overreacted. You see, we have some very delicate experiments set up in the lab. Rodrigo was afraid that you had disturbed them, and . . . What's this?"

He bent down to pick up an object lying in the grass. Justin's heart sank as he recognized his flashlight. Dr. Latour straightened up slowly. "And what, exactly, was this for?"

He spoke softly, but something in his voice made the twins press closer together. When neither answered, he took a step closer. "Answer me!" he commanded sharply.

Justin kept his mouth stubbornly shut, but Jenny answered truthfully enough, "We saw that the bars were loose and thought we'd take a look. We were just curious about what was in the lab. We didn't get inside."

The geologist pinched Jenny's chin with two strong fingers. Tilting her head back, he asked smoothly, "And what did you *see?*"

"Only . . . only burlap sacks." Jenny's voice trailed off at the menacing look in the two men's eyes.

"And they were taking pictures!" Rodrigo growled. He yanked the camera from Justin's hand. Opening the back with a violent jerk, he tore out the film that Justin had just replaced and trampled it into the ground.

"That settles it!" Dr. Latour snapped. "They're coming with us. I'll clear the stuff out of the lab. You get the kids in the jeep. And make sure you search them well first."

Without so much as another glance at the twins, he marched away. At the corner of the building, he turned. Pulling a small pistol from his pocket, he checked the safety catch and tossed it to Rodrigo. "Here! You may need this to keep the brats in line."

But Justin had seen his chance the instant Rodrigo turned his back to catch the gun. Dropping his sister's hand, he whispered urgently, "Run!"

They had only a few steps head start before angry shouts broke out behind them, but it was enough to bring Justin to the edge of the tall grass that lay between him and the DEA camp. A shot rang out, and he glanced backward as he dived under cover. To his dismay, he saw Jenny trip over Rodrigo's outstretched foot and sprawl on the ground. She seemed unhurt, and a moment later he heard her shout, "Let me go! You can't do this! Let me go!"

He hesitated only momentarily, wondering if he should go back and help, but it was enough to show him the tall figure of Dr. Latour rapidly closing the gap between them. In a fraction of a second, he made a decision. The only help available was at the DEA camp. He turned and ran.

His feet found the beaten-down path that led across the field to the DEA camp. Glancing over his shoulder, he saw that he was getting away from Dr. Latour as the tall geologist struggled through the thorny mass of bushes surrounding the lab. Elated, he settled into a running stride and saw his pursuer fall even farther behind. His heartbeat pounded loudly in his ears, but over it his mind repeated triumphantly, "I'm going to make it, I'm going to make it!"

He didn't know how many seconds had passed before he realized he was no longer moving away from Dr. Latour. The geologist was now through the brush and into the high grasses that covered most of the field. His powerful arms pushing aside the thick grass, he trotted at a diagonal toward the running boy.

Justin produced a desperate burst of speed, then his heart sank as he suddenly noticed what Dr. Latour was obviously well aware of. The path he had been following with such ease curved gradually to the right to avoid a patch of deeply rooted thorn bushes. It would lead him straight into Dr. Latour's waiting arms.

Justin swerved left into the briar patch. Thorns grabbed at his clothes as he dodged through tiny openings among the brambles. One long, sharp branch reached over his shoulder to slap him across the cheek, leaving a streak of red. Then the waving grain closed over his head. Grateful for the temporary shelter, he pushed deeper into the tangled grasses, using both hands as though he were wading in a chest-deep pool.

Sweat ran down his face, but he didn't dare stop to wipe it away. The notebook he had tucked inside his shirt rubbed against him, making it harder to run. *God, please don't let them hurt Jenny!* he pleaded silently. He stumbled over a root as his eyes suddenly blurred.

Now in the middle of the field, he could no longer see Dr. Latour. He was conscious only of the already glaring heat of the sun, an increasing fire in his chest, and a dusty-sweet scent that came from the drying grasses. He'd had this nightmare before, he suddenly realized—the one where you ran forever from some unseen enemy—only this time he couldn't seem to wake up.

He almost fell when his groping hands pushed ahead and met only air. Catching himself, he realized where he was. Here, a circular clearing had been clipped out of the grass, and in the center stood the grasshopper-like oil pump where he and Jenny had rested several days earlier. In the same instant, Justin also realized he had come far out of his way. The path he had followed and the metal roof of the DEA office now lay far to his right, even farther away than before.

Standing on tiptoe, Justin raised his head cautiously above the concealing brush. He froze as he caught sight of Dr. Latour standing directly between him and the safety of the DEA encampment. Head and shoulders above the surrounding grass, the tall geologist shielded his eyes with one hand as he scanned the field. Justin ducked down as Dr. Latour moved in his direction.

"Well, they won't get *these,* anyway!" Justin mumbled fiercely. Yanking the notebook from his belt, he slipped the roll of film into its plastic covering. Kneeling beside the oil pump, he thrust the bundle into a slight hollow behind one of the great iron legs. Certain that the package was invisible, he was up and across the other side of the clearing a few seconds later.

But he had lost much of his head start. Other oil pumps dotted the field here, and the grass grew only knee-high and not so thick. He lengthened his stride, but a shout from behind told him he had been seen. Glancing back, he saw that Dr. Latour too had broken through to the shorter grass. Running easily, he was now a scant thirty yards away.

It was then that Justin saw the other man. He stood at the edge of the field some distance away, where the grassland gave way to uncut jungle. Justin could only make out a vague form as sweat and a few tears blurred his vision. He turned his leaden legs in that direction as he croaked out a call for help. Whoever the man was, he might be able to assist Justin. It might even be someone from the DEA camp.

An answering shout rang out ahead of him. Wiping a

sunburned arm across his eyes, he pushed on as the distant man waved an arm in his direction. Then fresh horror gripped Justin as an all-too-familiar black leather jacket came into focus.

The man stood casually, watching the boy come closer. Freezing, Justin looked back frantically. Now even closer, Dr. Latour called out a command in Spanish, and Justin's new enemy pounded across the field.

For one long moment, Justin didn't move. A red haze danced before his eyes as he tried to draw air into his burning chest. His legs seemed incapable of carrying him any farther. His lips moved silently as he repeated desperately, "Please help me, God! Please help me!"

The haze cleared. He was looking straight at the tangled mass of the uncleared jungle only yards away. If he could only lose himself in there, he thought, he might still be able to circle around and reach the safety of the DEA camp. With new strength, he turned and ran for the shelter of the trees.

He could hear hoarse breathing close behind as he reached the edge of the field. Pushing Alan's many warnings out of his mind, he crashed through the underbrush, intent only on putting distance between himself and the two men who followed him. He was brought up short by a low, menacing growl.

Justin froze. Here, near the open fields, the trees were not the massive giants of the deep jungle, but they grew thick and close together. Their leafy canopies filtered the brilliant sun, letting through a dim green light that gave an illusion of coolness.

Just ahead, two small trees grew so close together that their branches interlocked to form a shady thicket. Emerging from the thicket, its heavy paws making no sound as it stepped gracefully around a massive fallen log, was an animal Justin recognized at once.

Muscles rippled under the short, yellow fur. The black circles that dotted the golden pelt blended with the earth and branches to make the long, sleek body seem a part of the dancing shadows and dim sunbeams. A heavy, cat-like head turned, finding Justin with an unblinking, golden-green stare. Justin suddenly remembered what Uncle Pete had told him about jaguars attacking defenseless human beings. Could the big animal sense his fear?

The jaguar paused, half in, half out of the thicket. The rumble of its low growl seemed to hold curiosity rather than anger. Without taking his eyes off the animal, Justin edged quietly backward. This new danger had temporarily driven his pursuers out of his mind. He stumbled over a dry branch, and a loud crack broke the silence. Justin's mouth went dry as the sleek muscles tensed under the smooth skin, and the low rumble rose to a roar.

A crash in the underbrush to his left diverted the animal's attention. The jaguar jerked its cat-like head around and sank back on its haunches as, some ten feet away, Dr. Latour lunged toward Justin.

"We've got him!" he called triumphantly. The steel-gray eyes narrowed as he took in Justin's frozen expression and realized that the boy hadn't even turned to look at him. Then he, too, caught sight of the jungle cat and froze in mid-step. The jaguar rose to four paws again and crouched down to face the geologist.

Another crackling in the brush, and the jaguar swung to Justin's right. Its muzzle pulled back in a snarl as the man in the black leather jacket broke into the open. The man took two long steps toward Justin, then his face twisted with terror as the golden-green eyes turned in his direction. Shaking, he stumbled back against a tree trunk.

This was the first time Justin had seen this man up close since they had boarded the boat two days earlier. The dark sunglasses were gone, and the thin face seemed yellower than ever. Drops of perspiration beaded his upper lip, but the man shivered in spite of the heat and the black leather jacket, His eyes, red and dilated, roved ceaselessly from side to side.

The fire in Justin's chest was easing, and he felt less fearful now that he stood face to face with this thin, shivering man who had frightened him so much. He didn't look strong enough to be a threat to anyone—much less a husky, athletic thirteen-year-old. It should be an easy matter to push past him and escape into the field while his two pursuers dealt with the jaguar, Justin thought. Justin took one small step to the right.

"Don't let him get away!" Justin realized with dismay that Dr. Latour had easily read his thoughts. The other man took a step toward Justin, an unpleasant grin stretching his thin lips. A wicked-looking knife appeared suddenly in one hand.

"I understand you've already met my old friend Choco," Dr. Latour spoke across the small clearing.

"So you *were* the one who had him follow us!" Justin said with a glare toward the geologist. "I knew it!"

Dr. Latour shrugged his shoulders. "He had strict orders to stay out of sight. But he's not too bright. They never are when they're this far gone on cocaine."

As Justin glanced at the tensed and waiting addict, Dr. Latour added, "He may not be bright but he's loyal—at least to anyone who will give him his daily cocaine ration. He'll cut you to pieces rather than let you by. In any case, there's no reason for you to run away. You and your sister will be released just as soon as Rodrigo and I are well away from here."

The hand he held out was long and slim, but Justin had already experienced the strength of that grip. "Now step over here quietly, and we'll get out of here. Unless you'd rather we left you to the jaguar!"

Justin stubbornly remained where he was. "You and Rodrigo are the cocaine dealers Special Agent Turner is looking for aren't you? I'll bet it was you who stole those files—and scared Jenny—just to get us to leave here!"

Dr. Latour looked amused. "Your uncle was getting too nosy. You wouldn't be in all this trouble if you'd left camp like we planned. You really messed up this operation!"

"And you burnt Eduardo's farm and house down!" Justin accused. "How could you do that? He wasn't hurting you!"

The look of amusement turned to annoyance. "What are you talking about?"

"You know, our friend's village! You burned it down because they wouldn't grow coca."

"Oh, yes, the village Choco told me about." Dr. Latour forced a friendly smile. "Look, kid, I just buy coca leaf from the local dealers. It's none of my business what they do to get it. I didn't hurt your friends. I'm just trying to make some money like a lot of other people."

"You'll never get away with it!" Justin answered defiantly. "Uncle Pete and Alan will be back anytime. They'll stop you!"

He glanced sideways at the crouching jaguar, shaking inwardly in spite of his brave words. The big cat seemed confused, its short tail lashing the ground as it swung its head from side to side as though trying to decide who to attack first. It didn't seem possible that scarcely two minutes had elapsed since Justin's wild dash into the jungle.

Dr. Latour laughed without humor. "Don't be a fool! We'll be out of here long before your busybody uncle gets back. This was our last haul anyway. And you and your sister are our insurance that no one tries to stop us."

He again reached out his hand. "Now step over here, and we'll leave while Choco distracts that animal."

Without moving, Justin looked at the geologist with disgust. "You'd just leave your friend to the jaguar while we get away?"

Dr. Latour was annoyed. "He'll get away just fine. Besides, he's just a drug addict. He's no good to anyone, and he won't last much longer anyway!"

Justin remembered the sadness in Mike's eyes when he talked of his sister. "Maybe he has a family somewhere that still cares about him," he said slowly.

"Well, I can promise he won't give you the same consideration," the geologist said dryly. Justin looked over at the addict. Catching his glance, the man stretched his thin lips in a crazed smile. Justin took an involuntary step backward. The geologist's voice sharpened suddenly. "Choco!"

Then everything happened at once. As Justin turned to make a final dash for escape, his leg became tangled in a vine. He sprawled backward just as the crazed addict lunged toward him, knife held high.

An ear-shattering roar drowned out the addict's sudden

terrified scream. The jaguar had finally made up his mind. Staring up helplessly, Justin saw the powerful muscles bunch up under the smooth yellow and black skin. Then he shut his eyes as the jaguar launched itself straight at him.

Chapter Eleven

JUNGLE CHASE

As JUSTIN braced himself for the impact of the jaguar's heavy body and sharp claws, the crack of a gunshot stung his ears. He didn't move for a long moment, then he let out his breath slowly and cautiously opened his eyes, scarcely able to believe that he was unhurt.

He felt his arms and legs. They were unmarked. Reassured, he freed himself from the vine that had tripped him and stood up. Glancing around, he saw the man Dr. Latour had called Choco slumped back against the moss-grown log, a faint pulse at his throat the only indication he was still alive. The jaguar lay unmoving across his chest.

There was no sight of the camp geologist, but Justin was vaguely aware of a crackling of dry twigs receding to his left. The loud thud of heavy boots jerked him around. He tensed for flight, then went limp with relief as Mike plunged into view, a 30/30 caliber hunting rifle over one shoulder.

Lowering the rifle to the ground, the young DEA agent leaned on it as he looked from Justin to the dead animal and back again. His chest still heaving from running, he demanded, "Are you okay, kid?"

When Justin nodded weakly, Mike leaned the rifle against a tree. Rolling the heavy body of the jaguar away from the unconscious cocaine addict, he examined the gunshot wound.

"A perfect head shot!" he announced as Justin knelt beside him. "There's a souvenir for you to take home, kid!"

He glanced aside at Justin, his expression still grim. "When I saw that cat going right for you . . . well, I didn't think I'd get a shot off in time!"

"Yeah, I guess you saved my life," Justin responded, eyeing the outstretched claws of the big cat with respect. "Thanks!"

Mike turned his attention to the unconscious man. Now that the jaguar had been rolled away, Justin could see that the black leather jacket was ripped to shreds where a vicious claw had raked down one arm. Long, shallow cuts stretched from the man's shoulder to his wrist.

"This guy really saved you!" he answered as he slipped a hand under the unconscious man's head. "I'd have been too late if he hadn't jumped in the way."

Lightly holding one skeletal wrist with a thumb and forefinger, he added, "He's really lucky! He must have knocked himself out against that log—he's got a lump the size of a baseball on the back of the head. But his pulse is strong, and that arm is only scratched."

He began to ease off the leather jacket. His eyes opened wide as he noticed the knife still clenched in Choco's fist. Twisting it loose, he motioned to the jaguar. "Was this for the cat . . . or for you?"

His question suddenly reminded Justin of the reason he was there. He jumped to his feet. "Mike, we've got to go!" he said urgently. "They're going to get away if we don't hurry!"

Mike glanced up at him sharply. "What are you talking about? *Who's* going to get away?"

Justin was almost dancing with impatience. "Dr. Latour and Rodrigo . . . they're the cocaine dealers! They made this guy follow us . . . and they took the cocaine . . . *and Jenny!* They're getting away with her!"

Leaving the now moaning Choco, Mike rose slowly to his feet. "Just a minute. Are you telling me you actually saw the cocaine?"

Putting a hand on Justin's shoulder, Mike looked into his eyes. "Look, kid, you aren't pulling my leg, are you?"

"No! I saw it! We both did! In the lab!" His words tumbled over each other as he poured out all that had happened since Mike had dropped them off the day before.

Mike stared at Justin uncertainly. "Are you trying to tell me that, after all our searching, you just happened to stumble over the leaders of the cocaine ring?"

Shaking his head in disbelief, he pulled a hand radio off his belt and barked out a few short orders in Spanish. Slapping Justin on the back, he said with admiration, "We send you home to keep you out of trouble, and instead you turn up a multi-million dollar cache of cocaine. Things sure do happen when you're around!"

He caught a motion at his feet. Choco, now fully conscious, was reaching feebly for the knife that still lay beside him on the ground. Kicking it out of his reach, Mike then tucked it into his own belt. "He'll keep until my men get here. Come on!"

Justin was still winded, but he followed Mike back across the oil field at a steady trot. Beyond the open field, he could already see several uniformed men running in their direction. As they slowed down to push through the thicker brush, he asked curiously, "Mike, how did you know I needed help?"

"I didn't!" Mike used his rifle to beat a path. "I was on my way over to see you—thought you might want an update on the raid yesterday. I took my rifle to do a little hunting.

"I've been out several times but never did see any big animals until today—and was cutting across the field back there when I heard that first roar. It's quite a coincidence that I happened to be passing through just when you ran into that jaguar."

"That was no 'coincidence,'" Justin answered soberly. "I prayed for help, and God sent you."

Mike looked at the boy strangely, but said nothing. They were now passing the oil pump where Justin had hidden the notebook and film. Justin paused to grab the package and stuff it inside his shirt, then broke into a run to catch up with the DEA agent.

As the buildings of the oil camp came into sight, Mike pulled Justin to a stop. "Take it easy!" he told the impatient boy. "I know you want to help your sister, but you can't just run out there. First, we'll take a quiet look around."

Pushing Justin behind him, he added firmly, "A *very* quiet look!"

There was no one in sight as they reached the cut lawn around the camp. Avoiding the lab, Mike silently led the way behind the closest bungalow. Crouching down at the corner, he whispered to Justin, "Stay here and keep out of trouble. I'll see if anyone's out there."

Justin opened his mouth to protest, but the roar of an engine drowned out his words. Before Mike could stop him, Justin was running around the corner. He reached the front of the bungalow just in time to see the camp jeep, with Dr. Latour at the wheel, careening through the open gate. As he reached the gravel driveway, one small figure in the front seat twisted around and waved frantically.

"Come back here!" Justin was running down the dusty track when Mike yanked him to a stop.

"Justin, I know how you feel." From the grim look on Mike's face, Justin knew he *did* understand. "But you'll do no good on foot. We'll have to use the helicopter. Come on! If they reach the cover of the jungle before we track them down, we'll never find them."

Following the footpath, Justin and Mike reached the DEA encampment just as two soldiers herded Choco into camp. He stumbled along, cradling his injured arm, but prodding machine guns at his back kept him moving. He had salvaged the torn leather jacket, which he held around his thin shoulders with his good arm. His black eyes glistened with hate as he caught sight of Justin and Mike.

Special Agent Turner met Mike and Justin outside the DEA office. Justin shifted impatiently from one foot to another while Mike rapidly updated the DEA agent. Before Mike had finished, the two DEA agents were already trotting briskly back toward the oil camp lab, Justin panting along behind. The rumbling of his stomach reminded him that he had missed breakfast.

Special Agent Turner glanced only briefly at the back window, where the metal bars still leaned against the wooden shutters, before heading around to the main door of the lab. To Justin's surprise, the lab door was unlocked. Special Agent Turner gave him a sharp look as he pushed it open.

Following the DEA agent and Mike inside, Justin blinked as his eyes adjusted to the sudden dimness. He looked around. The burlap bags he had glimpsed through the back window were gone. The big room looked much as it had on his first evening in camp. Then he noticed the empty space in the far corner where the sat-phone had been.

Special Agent Turner and Mike quickly searched the room. Straightening up at last from the tall file cabinet beside the door, the DEA agent said firmly, "This is just standard geological and lab equipment. I don't see a thing out of place."

"But there was!" Justin answered urgently. "There was a satellite phone right there on that counter—you know, the ones that look like a big briefcase. And there were a whole bunch of big sacks right there against the window. Jenny and I saw some little bags of white powder sitting on top—just like the stuff you showed us. They said they were going to 'haul' it all somewhere."

Special Agent Turner turned to Mike. "Did you actually see Dr. Latour in pursuit of Justin?"

"Well, no," Mike admitted. "I just saw the man my men hauled in. The kid says he's been following them. But I did see the camp jeep take off out of the gate mighty fast."

Special Agent Turner's usually smiling eyes were stern. "Justin, I know you've had a real scare with that jaguar, but this is quite an accusation you're bringing against Dr. Latour. He is a very well-known man with an excellent reputation."

"I'm telling the truth—I promise!" Justin insisted anxiously. "He said he was taking that sat-phone out of camp to call his men. He said you would be monitoring calls—something about being able to triangulate position, whatever that means."

"It means we can pinpoint the approximate area at ground level that a cell-phone or radio transmission originates," Mike explained.

"Then—didn't you hear anything?" Justin asked anxiously.

Justin held his breath as Special Agent Turner admitted, "Well, we did overhear one cell-phone transmission from this general area about an hour ago. Just a couple of hacienda owners talking prices on beef."

As Justin swallowed with disappointment, Mike spoke up. "That could have been a code, sir."

Justin looked up eagerly as Mike added, "I mean, I have been thinking. . . . Dr. Latour has had access to a helicopter! And he's got big-shot buddies all over the country. It would be the perfect setup, you have to admit!"

"Mike, I do know my job!" Special Agent Turner answered dryly. He looked down at Justin. "I'm not saying you're lying, Justin. I've given some thought to Dr. Latour myself. He does have both the know-how and connections to run an operation like this—as well as an available helicopter.

"But he also has a perfect record and a lot of very powerful friends in the Bolivian government. I told you before that there are government officials looking for any excuse to get us out of the country. If we call out a full-scale pursuit of Dr. Latour and he turns out to be clean, he'll have us thrown out of the country tomorrow. All our work would be down the drain."

He looked sternly down at Justin. "Justin, are you sure that was cocaine you saw and not a trick of your imagination?"

"Yes, I'm sure!" Justin cried. "Besides, he's got Jenny! And he's getting away with her! You believe me, Mike, don't you?"

Mike nodded. His drawl even broader than usual, he urged, "Sir, I'm sure the kid's telling the truth! We've finally got a chance to hit those drug traffickers hard. But we're going to lose them if we don't hurry!"

Justin and Mike both held their breath for a long moment, then Special Agent Turner nodded abruptly. "Okay, we'll go after them. But you'd better be right, Justin!"

Feeling as though he'd been running for a lifetime, Justin struggled to keep up with the two men as they headed back to the DEA encampment. The DEA agent was shouting out commands even before they reached the edge of the base, but by the time the helicopter was airborne, Dr. Latour had a full hour head start.

"They were heading north from camp," Mike informed Special Agent Turner as the older DEA agent settled himself into the copilot's seat. Behind him, semiautomatic weapons cradled across their knees, four men in battle fatigues sat straight-backed, their dark eyes watchful.

Looking down at Justin, who sat squeezed in between the two DEA agents, Mike added, "They'll leave the main road as soon as possible and try to lose us in the jungle. We'll have to pick them up before they leave the road."

Perched on the edge of the DEA agent's armrest, Justin kept his eyes on the narrow, dusty ribbon that whipped past below them. His reddish-brown eyebrows knit together in unconscious imitation of Uncle Pete as he wondered what was happening to Jenny.

"It's all my fault!" he said aloud. "If I'd stayed away from that lab, none of this would have happened."

"And they'd be getting clean away," Mike answered dryly. "Don't worry, kid. We'll get your sister back."

When Justin's gloomy expression didn't change, he added encouragingly. "Come on, Justin! You're the one who's been praying that we'd catch the drug dealers. Don't you believe what you preach?"

"Yeah, you're right!" Justin's face suddenly brightened as he caught sight of a moving, dust-colored cloud far ahead. "Hey, that must be them!"

As the helicopter gained on the moving cloud, they soon made out the tiny shape of an open jeep in the center of the billowing dust.

"We've got them now!" Mike announced triumphantly. But, as though in answer, the jeep suddenly swerved under the cover of trees. The young DEA agent struck the control board with his fist. "Blast it!"

Special Agent Turner spoke a few Spanish phrases into the microphone of the helicopter radio. "I relayed their last coordinates to the ground vehicles," he said to Justin. "But I'm afraid they will be long gone by the time our men get here."

"What are we going to do now?" Justin asked anxiously as they hovered over the spot where the jeep had disappeared.

"I suggest you do some more of your praying, kid," Mike answered grimly. "Finding them now will be like looking for a needle in a haystack!"

"There's no need to give up yet," Special Agent Turner said calmly. "They have to stick to some kind of track. We just need to find some indication of which direction they are heading. Mike, begin aerial search procedure."

Justin kept his eyes glued to the unbroken green canopy below as Mike swung the helicopter in ever-widening circles. There wasn't even the faint line against the trees that he had noticed when they had traced the road from the cocaine lab to the coca farm. If there was a road somewhere below them, it was no more than an undeveloped track.

They had been scanning the jungle for a full hour when Justin sat up with a jerk. "What's that?" he demanded excitedly, pointing out an open slash in the tangled mass of green, to the left of the wide circle that the helicopter was now tracing.

The clearing ahead was just like the many others he had seen during Mike's aerial surveillance flights. Thousands of similar clearings dotted the vast jungle area of the Beni where local inhabitants had hacked out small farms. They would cultivate their few crops until the poorly nourished soil gave out, then move on to begin the process all over somewhere else. This clearing had obviously been abandoned for some time, but what excited Justin was the faint line of a dirt track that angled across the overgrown fields.

"Couldn't that be the road they're on?" he asked eagerly.

"You could be right, kid!" Mike answered, a hint of excitement in his voice. "I'm going in for a closer look."

Just as Mike maneuvered over the abandoned fields, an open jeep bumped slowly onto the deeply rutted, overgrown track. "Look! There they are!" Justin called out.

As Mike dropped lower, Justin could make out three startled faces staring upward. Then a cloud of dust hid them from view as the jeep put on a burst of speed.

"We've got to stop them before they get to the other side!" Justin cried desperately.

But Mike was already acting. The tall weeds that had overtaken the field bent under a sudden violent wind, as Mike gently lowered the helicopter right into the path of the speeding vehicle. Justin saw Rodrigo slam against the windshield as the jeep slid to a stop.

Justin was already out of the helicopter and running. The four armed soldiers were close behind, surrounding the jeep before its occupants could move. Justin caught a glimpse of Dr. Latour, his arms held high and his narrow face tight with anger. Beside him, Rodrigo held a handkerchief to a cut on his forehead.

Jenny had instinctively grabbed the back of the seat to keep from following Rodrigo into the windshield. Now she climbed shakily over the seat and jumped to the ground. Hugging Justin tightly, she cried, "I knew you'd bring help!"

"I demand to know the meaning of this!" Dr. Latour protested as Special Agent Turner and Mike strode over to the jeep. His steel-gray eyes fastened on Justin. "What has this boy been telling you?"

"We have been informed that you are carrying cocaine," Special Agent Turner answered bluntly. But Justin had already scrambled to the back of the jeep.

"It's gone!" he cried in dismay.

"I don't know what you're talking about." Dr. Latour had recovered his usual self-confidence. He stepped out of the jeep. "We've been on a normal oil exploration trip. These kids have been pestering us for a ride. The boy ran off before we left, but we let the little girl come along with us."

Jenny gasped. "That's not true! You kidnapped me with a gun!"

Special Agent Turner reached under the front seat of the jeep and pulled out a semiautomatic rifle and the pistol Justin had seen earlier. "Do you always carry these weapons?"

"Of course!" Dr. Latour answered scornfully. "There are wild animals in these parts."

"If you're innocent, why did you run away?" Mike interrupted angrily. "You saw us chasing you all over the jungle!"

Dr. Latour looked down his long nose at the angry young agent. "Certainly I saw you. I assumed you were on one of your usual training maneuvers. Am I supposed to stop every time I see a helicopter overhead?"

Justin was still frantically searching the back of the jeep. "I know it was here! Wasn't it, Jenny?"

Jenny tugged on the DEA agent's arm. "There *was* cocaine back there—big bags of it. They were afraid you'd catch them so they dumped them—*and* that briefcase thing with the satellite phone in it!"

Her face fell. "They hid them awfully well, though, back in the trees. And they kept changing tracks. I don't think we could ever find it."

Dr. Latour's eyes swept over the twins. "These children are telling a pack of lies!" he said coldly. "You don't have one shred of evidence against me. Do you think anyone would believe their word against mine? I'll have your jobs for this!"

Special Agent Turner looked like a thundercloud. At his quick motion, the soldiers lowered their weapons and stepped back. His arms now at his sides, Dr. Latour smiled with satisfaction.

Dropping his gaze to the two children, Special Agent Turner said sharply, "Kids, if this is your idea of a practical joke . . ."

His hands clenched into fists, Mike muttered bitterly to Justin, "So this is the kind of help you get for praying! These guys are going to get away with this, and there's nothing we can do to stop them!"

But Justin had suddenly remembered something. He broke into a grin of relief. "Oh, no they won't!"

Reaching inside his shirt, he pulled out a small, rectangular package wrapped in plastic and handed it to Special Agent Turner. Turning to Dr. Latour, he said triumphantly, "You thought you'd destroyed the pictures we took of the cocaine in the lab, Dr. Latour, but you got the wrong roll of film! And I think Mr. Turner might be interested in this notebook we found under the back windowsill of the lab."

"Give me that, you little . . . !" Dr. Latour lunged toward Justin, but Mike stepped between them and strong hands grabbed Dr. Latour from behind.

Special Agent Turner seemed to get more meaning out of the small notebook than Justin had. As the DEA agent leafed through the pages, nodding with satisfaction, Mike burst out, "You're a well-known scientist, Dr. Latour. You've even won medals for helping other people. How could you do this?"

"Why not?" Dr. Latour sneered. "Where did my skills and goodwill get me? Another second-rate job in a third-rate country, making money for other people. I figured it was *my* turn to get rich!"

Mike scowled. "And I guess it didn't matter how many innocent people got hurt in the process!"

Turning away in disgust, Mike motioned to the soldiers. As two UMOPAR agents led him by the children, Dr. Latour glared down with hate, his usual self-confidence erased by defeat.

Chapter Twelve

SUCCESSFUL OPERATION

UNCLE PETE and Alan walked into the DEA base in search of the twins just as the handcuffed prisoners were being unloaded from the helicopter. Mike had stayed behind with a couple UMOPAR soldiers to drive the camp jeep back.

Much to Justin's disappointment, Uncle Pete only nodded with satisfaction when he learned that Dr. Latour and his assistant were the heads of an international cocaine ring.

"So that's it," was his only comment. After a brief conversation with Special Agent Turner, he ordered Justin and Jenny back to the oil camp.

"I'll be over as soon as possible to let you know how things turn out," Special Agent Turner promised the children. He gave Uncle Pete a strange look. "I have a few questions for Mr. Parker and Alan as well."

A few minutes later, the twins joined Uncle Pete and Alan on the dining veranda. Over a long overdue meal, they recounted all that had happened since Uncle Pete and Alan had lifted off that morning.

"After Justin got away and Dr. Latour went after him," Jenny explained, "Rodrigo made me help load the stuff from the lab into the jeep. He kept waving that gun around until I was sure it would go off. And here I thought he was such a nice guy!

"We had just finished when Dr. Latour came running up like he was being chased by hornets. Boy, was he angry! He said we had to get out of there fast, so Rodrigo shoved me into the front of the jeep. I was afraid Dr. Latour had hurt Justin, until I saw him running after us.

"I was praying that Justin would bring help. Then, just before we turned into the jungle, I heard a helicopter. But when we got under all those trees, I couldn't hear anything. I was getting pretty discouraged. The road was really bad, and the jeep was going so slowly that I thought of jumping out and running into the jungle. But they made me sit between them, and Rodrigo held onto my arm the whole time.

"Then they stopped to hide the sacks and satellite phone. They wouldn't let me see where they took the stuff, but it couldn't have been very far from the track. I thought maybe I could get away then, but they took turns watching me. A little while later, we drove out into that clearing and saw the helicopter. I was never so glad to see anyone in my life!"

When Jenny finished her story, Uncle Pete shook his head in disbelief. "It seems I can't leave you two alone without you tumbling into some kind of trouble!"

He eyed them sternly. "I thought you promised to let me know before you started chasing bad guys again."

"We *were* going to tell you, Uncle Pete!" Justin protested. "But you took off so fast this morning, we didn't get a chance! Anyway, we didn't really know anything for sure—just what we overheard.

We thought we'd better check it out before accusing anyone of anything."

"Next time, try jumping out of bed a little faster." Uncle Pete responded dryly. But there was a twinkle in his eye as he added, "Given the circumstances, I must admit I would have done the same thing."

He was interrupted as the camp jeep, with Mike at the wheel, roared into the gravel driveway and braked to a stop at the edge of the veranda. Mike hopped out, waving his arms excitedly. The bitterness that had lined his face was gone. As Special Agent Turner stepped out on the passenger side, Mike announced jubilantly, "We found the cocaine! Every last bit of it!"

Running up the steps, Mike clapped Justin on the shoulder. "That stuff was so well hidden, we'd never have found it on our own. It was Justin's evidence that did it. When Rodrigo saw that we had the notebook and film, he just collapsed and told us all he knew. His directions led us right to the cocaine."

As Justin turned red with pleasure and embarrassment, Special Agent Turner, who had followed Mike onto the veranda, pulled out a chair and sat down. Leaning forward, he fastened keen gray eyes on Uncle Pete. "Mr. Parker, you don't seem too surprised by the arrest of two of your key personnel. Why? Did you have some idea of what was going on?"

Uncle Pete shook his head. "No, I had no idea that Dr. Latour and Rodrigo were involved in drug trafficking. But I wasn't too surprised to find out. I knew that *something* strange was going on here."

"What do you mean by that?" Special Agent Turner asked, raising an eyebrow.

Uncle Pete tilted his chair back against the wall as he responded, "I was sent here because we had received reports that the oil discovered here had turned out to be too low-grade and in too small quantities to be worth developing. The samples Dr. Latour sent in confirmed his reports. This was surprising, as earlier reports had indicated a large reserve of high-grade oil. But it wasn't the first time preliminary reports had proven overly optimistic."

As he paused, Alan explained, "Because of Dr. Latour's reports, we shut down the oil pumps and dismissed the workers. He's been out ever since prospecting for other possible oil sites—or so we thought!"

"You mean he wasn't looking for oil all those times that he took out the helicopter?" Jenny interrupted eagerly.

Uncle Pete held up a hand for silence. "I came down here with the intention of shutting down the whole camp. When I arrived, I reviewed Dr. Latour's reports as a matter of course. They were very well done, but I never take reports at face value. So I took a few samples of my own.

"I've been around oil long enough to know high-grade oil when I see it. I sent the samples to Santa Cruz for processing, then decided to check out the fieldwork Dr. Latour claimed to have done in the last few months. I informed Dr. Latour that I would be flying out to inspect his survey sites, and, of course, you know that the office was robbed the next day."

Uncle Pete smiled with satisfaction as he pulled a small notebook out of his breast pocket. "What Dr. Latour didn't know is that I have a habit of jotting down any information pertinent to my investigation. By that time, I was quite sure Dr. Latour had been falsifying his reports. The robbery of the office files was just too convenient, and he was too determined to get me out of camp. What I couldn't figure out was why!

"Anyway, Alan and I decided to check out his surveys of promising oil fields on our own, using the coordinates I had jotted down. We discovered that there *were* no so-called 'survey sites.' In fact, one set of coordinates put us smack in the middle of a river. We planned to confront him today, but of course, you got to him first."

"It never occurred to me to check up on Dr. Latour's lab reports and field explorations," Alan added gloomily. "After all, I'm no geologist, and Dr. Latour is one of the best in his field. He must have taken those fake samples from other oil sites around the area. What I can't figure out is what he was doing all those weeks that he had the helicopter out. He couldn't have just been flying out to the cocaine lab and back."

"I can answer that!" Mike announced from his perch on the veranda railing. "Rodrigo has agreed to testify against Dr. Latour, who was head of the drug ring, in return for a lighter sentence. He has admitted that they were using the helicopter to ferry the cocaine to a friend with a large estate near Santa Cruz. Those times that they didn't check in on the UHF radio when they were out in the field, they were in Santa Cruz—not checking out oil sites around here."

"It wasn't that drug lord you told us about, was it?" Justin asked eagerly. "The one with his own airplane and everything?"

Mike grinned broadly. "That's right. Between Rodrigo's confession and the information in that notebook you found, the UMOPAR has managed to put *him* under arrest as well."

"So their so-called 'exploration trips' were a cover-up for their drug dealings," Special Agent Turner commented thoughtfully. "It gave them a reason for traveling in the jungle without arousing any suspicions. I imagine Dr. Latour faked those samples because he didn't want the area swarming with oil crews."

Mike spoke up again. "Rodrigo has admitted that they had Choco, one of their drug contacts, follow you. Choco put the tarantula in the outhouse, too. And they faked the robbery the other day. We found Alan's missing cuff links and radio tossed into the bushes behind the lab. They wanted to get the Parkers out of camp so they could get this last payload of cocaine out."

Justin couldn't contain his curiosity any longer. "What about the notebook I found? Did you discover what was in it?"

"We sure did!" Special Agent Turner answered with satisfaction. "That notebook is the most important haul we've made yet. It was written in code, but we had no trouble breaking it, once we fed the contents into the computer. It contains names and information about people involved in the drug traffic, as well as dates and details of cocaine shipments. We'll turn that information over to the UMOPAR—at least that relating to Bolivian nationals."

"What's going to happen to Dr. Latour and Rodrigo now?" Jenny asked.

"They'll be sent to the U.S. for trial," Special Agent Turner answered. "It seems that Rodrigo took out U.S. citizenship during his years in Miami. So he, too, will have to stand trial in U.S. courts. No clever lawyers are going to get them off this time."

Mike turned to Justin. "Your pictures turned out beautifully. With those and the other evidence we've collected, we have a clear case against the two of them."

"I've got just one more question," Justin said. "Whatever happened to that lab we found in the jungle?"

Mike laughed. "That's right! I was on my way to tell you about that when things got crazy this morning. UMOPAR men are removing all the equipment and chemicals for evidence. Then the place will be burned to the ground. That's one cocaine lab that will never be used again!"

Special Agent Turner stood up. "Mike and I had better be on our way. We have a lot to do. We've finished our training operation here, and it has been a bigger success than we ever dreamed it would be. But there are still cocaine rings in other places to go after. We're moving out in two days."

Standing up, Mike looked down at Justin and Jenny. "Maybe you were right about good winning out in the end. At any rate, we owe you kids a lot!"

Jenny shook her head. "We didn't really do anything!"

"I suppose you're going to tell me it was God," Mike answered with a skeptical twist of the lips. But his tone was thoughtful this time, not mocking.

Special Agent Turner shook hands all around. Stopping at Justin, he said briskly, "You have quite an eye for digging out information, Justin. Why don't you look me up in a few years? There will always be a place for you on my team!"

As he shook Uncle Pete's hand, Uncle Pete said, "We will be pulling out of here as well—tomorrow morning, in fact. My job is done, and it's time to be heading home. Right, kids?"

Jenny frowned. "I admit, I'll be glad to say good-bye to the wildlife!"

Everyone chuckled, but Justin wondered how he would ever

settle down to suburban Seattle after all the excitement of the last couple of weeks.

Special Agent Turner turned to Alan. "I suppose you will be moving out as well, if the oil camp is shutting down."

Alan grinned. "Maybe not. We should be hearing back from Santa Cruz any time on those samples we sent in. If they prove as profitable as Mr. Parker thinks, this camp may be booming again."

The next morning, Justin sorted through his belongings. Picking up his Bible, he leafed through the pages. It was a very nice Bible, with colorful maps and interesting charts and facts about Bible times in the back. Laying it aside, he shoved the rest of his clothes into the suitcase.

By breakfast time, all three Parkers were packed and ready for the two-hour drive into Trinidad. They would fly out to Santa Cruz later that morning, where Uncle Pete planned to buy tickets to Miami. Justin was loading suitcases into the back of the jeep when he saw Mike hurrying across the driveway. The tall DEA agent was carrying a heavy-duty plastic garbage sack, the opening knotted tightly.

"Just thought I'd see you off," he commented briefly, casually dropping the garbage sack on top of the other luggage.

Alan dropped the group off at the airport on the outskirts of Trinidad. It consisted of a galvanized-metal warehouse that had been converted into a terminal, with a single strip of asphalt runway. As they unloaded the luggage, Mike swung the black plastic sack over his shoulder.

"Your plane won't be in for another hour," Alan informed Uncle Pete. "I'm going to make a quick run to the post office. I'm hoping the results of those oil samples are in by now. I'll be back in time to see you off."

With Mike's help, Uncle Pete checked their luggage in at the long table that served as a checking counter. Alan still hadn't returned by the time the boarding of flight 903 to Santa Cruz was announced. Most of the passengers had filed out the double doors that led to the waiting forty-passenger DC-3 prop plane, when Uncle Pete finally declared that they would have to leave.

The last call for boarding echoed from massive loudspeakers near the vaulted metal ceiling. Reluctantly, the twins turned to say good-bye to Mike, who still carried the plastic garbage sack over his shoulder.

"I wanted you to have this to remember us by," Justin told him somewhat hesitantly.

He handed Mike a newspaper-wrapped package. Mike unwrapped it and held up Justin's Bible. Quickly leafing through it, he looked curiously at Justin. "Well, kid, knowing you has certainly made me wonder if maybe there is a God out there controlling things. I promise I'll read it."

He lowered the garbage sack to the floor. "I've got something for you, too, kids. Not that I think you'll ever forget the last few days." Untying the sack, he dumped out a rolled-up bundle of fur that glinted gold and black in the fluorescent lights that illuminated the dim warehouse.

"It's the jaguar skin!" Justin exclaimed.

Mike grinned. "I promised you could have it as a souvenir.

It's been salted down, but you'll have to cure it when you get home."

Handing Justin an official-looking envelope, he explained briefly, "Under normal circumstances, you aren't allowed to hunt jaguar. This gives you permission to take the pelt through customs."

Jenny gently stroked the kitten-soft fur. "It's beautiful!"

A flight attendant in a spotless blue and gold uniform was now frantically waving at the group from the wide double doors that led to the runway. Calling a final good-bye, the twins followed Uncle Pete across the asphalt to where the plane waited, its jet engines roaring impatiently. Justin looked back to see Mike still watching them. He smiled and waved again and held up the Bible Justin had given him.

They were climbing the steep staircase that led into the airplane when they heard running footsteps behind them. Alan hurried up the staircase, waving an envelope. "It came!" he panted. "The sample results. That field behind the oil camp is rich with high-grade oil! I'll have the work crews move in next week."

He handed Uncle Pete a slip of paper. "There was an e-mail for you, too. I printed it out."

Uncle Pete unfolded the sheet of computer paper. He read aloud: *Good work on the Beni job. Since you are already down there, I'm sure you won't mind another short stop on your way home. A minor problem has developed in the Triton field office in Bogotá, Colombia. I have already taken the liberty of revising your travel itinerary. You may pick up your new tickets at the American Airlines desk in Santa Cruz.*

He glanced up. "It's signed by my boss in Washington. I sent him a lengthy e-mail last night. How about it, kids? Would you mind just one more stop before we head home?"

The twins' ear-to-ear grins were all the answer he needed.

The flight attendant, standing in the doorway of the plane, waved again. She now looked distinctly annoyed. The twins hurried up the stairs behind Uncle Pete and followed him to the back of the plane. The plane was soon taxiing down the runway.

Justin checked his seat number and slid into a window seat. Belting herself in beside him, Jenny chattered, "I wonder what Bogotá will be like. It's supposed to be as big as New York City. The jungle was interesting, but it'll be nice to see a real city again."

Justin was listening with only one ear. As the plane soared into the air, he exclaimed, "Take a look over there!"

Jenny leaned over to peer out the small, round window. Like an endless, wave-tossed green sea, the vast tangle of the Beni jungle stretched below them as far as they could see. Far off to their left, a column of smoke billowed high above the trees—all that was left of the cocaine lab that had produced so much wealth and misery.

The two children watched as the column of smoke grew fainter and fainter. The plane banked right, and the last reminder of their jungle adventure faded out of sight.

CAVE OF THE INCA RE

Catch the Parker Twins in another adventure.

The Cave of the Inca Re is cursed. Anyone who goes in comes out completely crazy . . . if they come out at all.

Traveling with their uncle to Bolivia sounded awesome to Jenny and Justin Parker. But when they discover some greedy smugglers, the twins find themselves in a deadly situation where their only escape is the dangerous Cave of the Inca Re.

Is God strong enough to save them from the curse?

ISBN: 0-8254-4145-5